INTERNATIONAL

Invitation
to a
Beheading

Invitation to a Beheading

VLADIMIR NABOKOV

TRANSLATED BY DMITRI NABOKOV
in collaboration with the author

VINTAGE INTERNATIONAL
Vintage Books
A Division of Random House, Inc.
New York

First Vintage International Edition, September 1989

Copyright © 1959 by Vladimir Nabokov

All rights reserved under International and Pan-American Copyright Conventions. Published in the United States by Vintage Books, a division of Random House, Inc., New York. Originally published, in hardcover, by G.P. Putnam's Sons, New York, in 1959. This edition is published by arrangement with the Estate of Vladimir Nabokov.

Library of Congress Cataloging-in-Publication Data
Nabokov, Vladimir, 1899–1977.
  [Priglashenie na kazn'. English]
  Invitation to a beheading / Vladimir Nabokov; translated by
Dmitri Nabokov in collaboration with the author. — 1st Vintage
international ed.
    p. cm.
  Translation of: Priglashenie na kazn'.
  ISBN 0-679-72531-8 (pbk.) : $7.95
  I. Title.
PG3476.N3P73 1989
891.73'42—dc20   89-40148
                                              CIP

Manufactured in the United States of America
579B864

To Véra

Foreword

The Russian original of this novel is entitled *Priglashenie na kazn'*. Notwithstanding the unpleasant duplication of the suffix, I would have suggested rendering it as *Invitation to an Execution*; but, on the other hand, *Priglashenie na otsechenie golovï* ("Invitation to a Decapitation") was what I really would have said in my mother tongue, had I not been stopped by a similar stutter.

I composed the Russian original exactly a quarter of a century ago in Berlin, some fifteen years after escaping from the Bolshevist regime, and just before the Nazi regime reached its full volume of welcome. The question whether or not my seeing both in terms of one dull beastly farce had any effect on this book, should concern the good reader as little as it does me.

Priglashenie na kazn' came out serially in a Russian émigré magazine, the *Sovremenniya Zapiski*, appearing in Paris, and later, in 1938, was published in that city by the *Dom Knigi*. Emigré reviewers, who were puzzled but liked it, thought they distinguished in it a "Kafkaesque" strain, not knowing that I had no German, was completely ignorant of modern German literature, and had not yet read any French or English translations of Kafka's works. No doubt, there do exist certain stylistic links between this book and, say, my earlier stories (or my later *Bend Sinister*); but there are none between it and *Le chateau* or *The Trial*. Spiritual affinities have no place in my concept of literary criticism, but if I did have to choose a kindred soul, it would certainly be that great artist rather than G. H. Orwell or other popular purveyors of illustrated ideas and publicistic fiction. Incidentally, I could never understand why every book of mine invariably sends reviewers scurrying in search of more or less celebrated names for the purpose of passionate comparison. During the last three decades they have hurled at me (to list but a few of these harmless missiles) Gogol, Tolstoevski, Joyce, Voltaire, Sade, Stendhal, Balzac, Byron, Bierbohm, Proust, Kleist, Makar Marinski, Mary McCarthy, Meredith (!), Cervantes, Charlie Chaplin, Baroness Murasaki, Pushkin, Ruskin, and even Sebastian Knight. One author, however, has never been mentioned in this connection—the only author whom I must gratefully recognize as an influence upon me at the time of writing this book; namely, the melancholy, extravagant, wise, witty, magical, and altogether delightful Pierre Delalande, whom I invented.

If some day I make a dictionary of definitions wanting

single words to head them, a cherished entry will be "To abridge, expand, or otherwise alter or cause to be altered, for the sake of belated improvement, one's own writings in translation." Generally speaking the urge to do this grows in proportion to the length of time separating the model from the mimic; but when my son gave me to check the translation of this book and when I, after many years, had to reread the Russian original, I found with relief that there was no devil of creative emendation for me to fight. My Russian idiom, in 1935, had embodied a certain vision in the precise terms that fitted it, and the only corrections which its transformation into English could profit by were routine ones, for the sake of that clarity which in English seems to require less elaborate electric fixtures than in Russian. My son proved to be a marvelously congenial translator, and it was settled between us that fidelity to one's author comes first, no matter how bizarre the result. *Vive le pédant,* and down with the simpletons who think that all is well if the "spirit" is rendered (while the words go away by themselves on a naïve and vulgar spree—in the suburbs of Moscow for instance—and Shakespeare is again reduced to play the king's ghost).

My favorite author (1768-1849) once said of a novel now utterly forgotten "*Il a tout pour tous. Il fait rire l'enfant et frissonner la femme. Il donne à l'homme du monde un vertige salutaire et fait rêver ceux qui ne rêvent jamais.*" *Invitation to a Beheading* can claim nothing of the kind. It is a violin in a void. The worldling will deem it a trick. Old men will hurriedly turn from it to regional romances and the lives of public figures. No clubwoman will thrill. The evil-minded will perceive in little Emmie a sister of little Lolita, and the disciples of the Viennese witch-doctor will snigger over it in their grotesque world of communal guilt and *progresivnoe* education. But (as the author of *Discours sur les ombres* said in reference to another lamp-light): I know (*je connais*) a few (*quelques*) readers who will jump up, ruffling their hair.

Oak Creek Canyon, Arizona

June 25, 1959

Invitation
to a
Beheading

COMME UN FOU SE CROIT DIEU,

NOUS NOUS CROYONS MORTELS.

—Delaland: *Discours sur les ombres*

One

In accordance with the law the death sentence was announced to Cincinnatus C. in a whisper. All rose, exchanging smiles. The hoary judge put his mouth close to his ear, panted for a moment, made the announcement and slowly moved away, as though ungluing himself. Thereupon Cincinnatus was taken back to the fortress. The road wound around its rocky base and disappeared under the gate like a snake in a crevice. He was calm; however, he had to be supported during the journey through the long corridors, since he planted his feet unsteadily, like a child who has just learned to walk, or as if he were about to fall through like a man who has dreamt that he is walking on water only to have a sudden doubt: but is this possible?

Rodion, the jailer, took a long time to unlock the door of Cincinnatus' cell—it was the wrong key—and there was the usual fuss. At last the door yielded. Inside, the lawyer was already waiting. He sat on the cot, shoulder-deep in thought, without his dress coat (which had been forgotten on a chair in the courtroom—it was a hot day, a day that was blue all through); he jumped impatiently when the prisoner was brought in. But Cincinnatus was in no mood for talking. Even if the alternative was solitude in this cell, with its peephole like a leak in a boat—he did not care, and asked to be left alone; they all bowed to him and left.

So we are nearing the end. The right-hand, still untasted part of the novel, which, during our delectable reading, we would lightly feel, mechanically testing whether there were still plenty left (and our fingers were always gladdened by the placid, faithful thickness) has suddenly, for no reason at all, become quite meager: a few minutes of quick reading, already downhill, and—O horrible! The heap of cherries, whose mass had seemed to us of such a ruddy and glossy black, had suddenly become discrete drupes: the one over there with the scar is a little rotten, and this one has shriveled and dried up around its stone (and the very last one is inevitably hard and unripe) O horrible! Cincinnatus took off his silk jerkin, put on his dressing gown and, stamping his feet a little to stop the shivering, began walking around the cell. On the table glistened a clean sheet of paper and, distinctly outlined against this whiteness, lay a beautifully sharpened pencil, as long as the life of any man except Cincinnatus, and with an ebony gleam to each of its six facets. An enlightened descendant of the index finger. Cincinnatus wrote: "In spite of everything I am comparatively.

After all I had premonitions, had premonitions of this finale." Rodion was standing on the other side of the door and peering with a skipper's stern attention through the peephole. Cincinnatus felt a chill on the back of his head. He crossed out what he had written and began shading gently; an embryonic embellishment appeared gradually and curled into a ram's horn. O horrible! Rodion gazed through the blue porthole at the horizon, now rising, now falling. Who was becoming seasick? Cincinnatus. He broke out in a sweat, everything grew dark, and he could feel the rootlet of every hair. A clock struck—four or five times—with the vibrations and re-vibrations, and reverberations proper to a prison. Feet working, a spider—official friend of the jailed—lowered itself on a thread from the ceiling. No one, however, knocked on the wall, since Cincinnatus was as yet the sole prisoner (in such an enormous fortress!).

Sometime later Rodion the jailer came in and offered to dance a waltz with him. Cincinnatus agreed. They began to whirl. The keys on Rodion's leather belt jangled; he smelled of sweat, tobacco and garlic; he hummed, puffing into his red beard; and his rusty joints creaked (he was not what he used to be, alas—now he was fat and short of breath). The dance carried them into the corridor. Cincinnatus was much smaller than his partner. Cincinnatus was light as a leaf. The wind of the waltz made the tips of his long but thin mustache flutter, and his big limpid eyes looked askance, as is always the case with timorous dancers. He was indeed very small for a full-grown man. Marthe used to say that his shoes were too tight for her. At the bend in the corridor stood another guard, nameless, with a rifle and wearing a doglike mask with a gauze mouthpiece. They described a circle near him and glided back into the cell, and now Cincinnatus regretted that the swoon's friendly embrace had been so brief.

With banal dreariness the clock struck again. Time was advancing in arithmetical progression: it was now eight. The ugly little window proved accessible to the sunset; a fiery parallelogram appeared on the side wall. The cell was filled to the ceiling with the oils of twilight, containing extraordinary pigments. Thus one would wonder, is that some reckless colorist's painting there to the right of the door, or another window, an ornate one of a kind that already no longer exists? (Actually it was a parchment sheet hanging on the wall with two columns of detailed "rules for prisoners"; the bent corner, the red letters of the heading, the vignettes, the ancient seal of the city—namely, a furnace with wings—provided the necessary materials for the evening illumination.) The cell's quota of furniture consisted of a table, a chair and the cot. Dinner (those condemned to death were entitled to get the same meals as the wardens) had already been standing and growing cold on its zinc tray for a long time. It grew quite dark. Suddenly the place was filled with golden, highly-concentrated electric light.

Cincinnatus lowered his feet from the cot. A bowling ball rolled through his head, diagonally from nape to temple; it paused and started back. Meanwhile the door opened and the prison director entered.

He was dressed as always in a frock coat and held himself exquisitely straight, chest out, one hand in his bosom, the other behind his back. A perfect toupee, black as pitch, and with a waxy parting, smoothly covered his head. His face, selected without love, with its thick sallow cheeks and somewhat obsolete system of wrinkles, was enlivened in a sense by two, and only by two, bulging eyes. Moving his legs evenly in his columnar trousers, he strode from the wall to the table, almost to the cot—but, in spite of his majestic solidity, he calmly vanished, dissolving into the air. A minute later, however, the door opened once again, this time with the familiar grating sound, and, dressed as always in a frock coat, his chest out, in came the same person.

"Having learned from trustworthy sources that your fate has been sort of sealed," he began in a fruity bass, "I have deemed it my duty, dear sir . . ."

Cincinnatus said: "Kind. You. Very." (This still had to be arranged.)

"You are very kind," said an additional Cincinnatus, having cleared his throat.

"Mercy," exclaimed the director, unmindful of the tactlessness of that word. "Mercy! Think nothing. Duty. I always. But why, may I be so bold as to ask, have you not touched your food?"

The director removed the cover and raised to his sensitive nose the bowl of coagulated stew. He took a potato with two fingers and began to chew powerfully, already picking out with an eyebrow something on another dish.

"I do not know what better food you could want," he said with displeasure, and, shooting out his cuffs, sat down at the table so as to be more comfortable while eating the rice pudding.

Cincinnatus said: "I should like to know if it will be long now."

"Excellent sabayon! Should still like to know if it will be long now. Unfortunately I myself do not know. I am always informed at the last moment; I have complained many times and can show you all the correspondence on the subject if you are interested."

"So it may be tomorrow morning?" asked Cincinnatus.

"If you are interested," said the director, ". . . Yes, downright delicious and most satisfying, that is what I'll tell you. And now, *pour la digestion*, allow me to offer you a cigarette. Have no fear, at most this is only the one before last," he added wittily.

"It is not out of curiosity that I ask," said Cincinnatus. "It is true that cowards are always inquisitive. But I assure you . . . Even if I can't control my chills and so forth—that does not mean anything. A rider is not responsible for the shivering of his horse. I want to know why for this reason: the compensation for a death sentence is knowledge of the exact hour when one is to die. A great luxury, but one that is well earned. However, I am being left in that ignorance which is tolerable only to those living at liberty. And furthermore, I have in my head many projects that were begun and interrupted at various times . . . I simply shall not pursue them if the time remaining before my execution is not sufficient for their orderly conclusion. This is why . . ."

"Oh, will you please stop mumbling," the director said irritably. "In the first place, it is against the rules, and in the second—I am telling you in plain Russian and for the second time—I do not know. All I can tell you is that your fate-mate is expected to arrive any day now; and when he does arrive, and has rested, and got used to the surroundings, he will still have to test the instrument, if, of course, he has not brought his own, which is altogether likely. How's the tobacco? Not too strong?"

"No," answered Cincinnatus, after looking absent-mind-edly at his cigarette. "Only it seems to me that according to the law . . . not you, perhaps, but the administrator of the city . . . is supposed to . . ."

"We've had our chat, and that will do," said the director. "Actually I came here not to listen to complaints but to . . ." Blinking, he rummaged first in one pocket, then in another; finally from an inside breast pocket he produced a sheet of ruled paper, obviously torn from a school note-book.

"There is no ash tray here," he observed, gesturing with his cigarette; "oh well, let us drown it in what's left of the rest of this sauce . . . So. I would say the light is a bit harsh. Maybe if we . . . Oh, never mind; it will have to do."

He unfolded the paper and, without putting on his horn-rimmed glasses, but holding them in front of his eyes, he began to read distinctly:

" 'Prisoner! In this solemn hour, when all eyes' . . . I think we had better stand," he interrupted himself with concern and rose from his chair. Cincinnatus also rose.

" 'Prisoner, in this solemn hour, when all eyes are upon thee, and thy judges are jubilant, and thou art preparing for those involuntary bodily movements that directly fol-low severance of the head, I address to thee a parting word. It is my lot—and this I will never forget—to provide thy sojourn in gaol with all that multitude of comforts which the law allows. I shall therefore be glad to devote all pos-sible attention to any expression of thy gratitude, preferably, however, in written form and on one side of the sheet.' "

"There," said the director, folding his glasses. "That will

be all. I shall not keep you any longer. Let me know if you should need anything."

He sat down at the table and began to write rapidly, thus indicating that the audience was over. Cincinnatus went out.

On the corridor wall dozed the shadow of Rodion, hunched over on the shadow of a stool, with only a fringe of beard outlined in rufous. Further on, at the bend in the wall, the other guard had taken off his uniform mask and was wiping his face with his sleeve. Cincinnatus started down the stairs. The stone steps were narrow and slippery, with the impalpable spiral of a ghostly railing. Upon reaching the bottom he again went along corridors. A door with the sign "office" in mirrorlike inversion was wide open; moonlight glistened on an inkwell and a wastebasket rustled and rattled furiously under the table: a mouse must have fallen into it. Cincinnatus, after passing many other doors, stumbled, hopped, and found himself in a small courtyard, filled with various parts of the dismantled moon. This night the password was silence, and the soldier at the gate responded with silence to Cincinnatus' silence and let him pass; likewise at all the other gates. Leaving behind the misty mass of the fortress he began to slide down a steep, dewy bank of turf, reached a pale path between cliffs, twice, three times crossed the bends of the main road—which, having finally shaken off the last shadow of the fortress, ran more straight and free—and a filigrane bridge across a dried-up rivulet brought Cincinnatus to the city. He climbed to the top of a steep incline, turned left on Garden Street, and sped past a shrubbery in grayish bloom. A lighted window flashed somewhere; behind some fence a dog shook its chain but did not bark. The breeze was doing all it could to cool the fugitive's bare neck. Now and then a wave of fragrance would come from the Tamara Gardens. How well he knew that public park! There, where Marthe, when she was a bride, was frightened of the frogs and cockchafers... There, where, whenever life seemed unbearable, one could roam, with a meal of chewed lilac bloom in one's mouth and firefly tears in one's eyes... That green turfy tamarack park, the languor of its ponds, the tum-tum-tum of a distant band... He turned on Matterfact Street, past the ruins of an ancient factory, the pride of the town, past whispering lindens, past the festive-looking white bungalows of the telegraph employees, perpetually celebrating somebody's birthdate, and came out on Telegraph Street. From there a narrow lane went uphill, and again the lindens began to murmur discreetly. Two men, supposedly on a bench, were quietly conversing in the obscurity of a public garden. "I say he's wrong," said one. The other replied unintelligibly, and both gave a kind of sigh which blended naturally with the sough of the foliage. Cincinnatus ran out into a circular plaza where the moon stood watch over the familiar statue of a poet that looked like a snowman—a cube for a head, legs stuck together—and, after a few more pattering steps, was in his own street. On the right the moon cast dissimilar patterns of branches on the walls of similar houses, so that it was only by the expression of the shadows, by the interciliary bar between two windows that Cincinnatus recognized his own house. Marthe's top-floor window was dark but open. The children must be sleeping on the hook-nosed balcony—there was a glimpse of something white there. Cincinnatus ran up the front steps, pushed open the door, and entered his lighted cell. He turned around, but already he was locked in. O horrible! The pencil glistened on the table. The spider sat on the yellow wall.

"Turn off the light!" shouted Cincinnatus.

His observer through the peephole turned it off. Darkness and silence began to merge but the clock interfered; it struck eleven times, thought for a moment, and struck once more, and Cincinnatus lay supine gazing into the dark, where bright dots were scattering and gradually disappearing. Darkness and silence merged completely. It was then and only then (that is, lying supine on a prison cot, after midnight, after a horrible, horrible, I simply cannot tell you what a horrible day) that Cincinnatus C. clearly evaluated his situation.

At first, against the background of that black velvet which lines at night the underside of the eyelids, Marthe's face appeared as in a locket; her doll-like rosiness; her shiny forehead with its childlike convexity; her thin eyebrows, slanting upward, high above her round hazel eyes. She began to blink, turning her head, and there was a black velvet ribbon on her soft, creamy-white neck, and the velvety quiet of her dress flared at the bottom, blending with the darkness. That is how he saw her among the audience, when they led him up to the freshly painted defendants' bench on which he did not dare sit, but stood beside it (and still he got emerald paint all over his hands, and the newspaper men greedily photographed the fingerprints he had left on the back of the bench). He could see their tense foreheads, he could see the gaudy pantaloons of the fops, and the hand-mirrors and iridescent scarves of the women of fashion; but the faces were indistinct—of all the spectators he remembered only round-eyed Marthe. The defense counsel and the prosecutor, both wearing makeup and looking very much alike (the law required that they be uterine brothers but such were not always available, and then makeup was used), spoke with virtuoso rapidity the five thousand words allotted to each. They spoke alternately and the judge, following the rapid exchanges, would move his head, right and left and all the other heads followed suit; only Marthe, half-turned, sat motionless like an astonished child, her gaze fixed on Cincinnatus, standing next to the bright green park bench. The defense counsel, an advocate of classic decapitation, won easily over the inventive prosecutor, and the judge summed up the case.

Fragments of these speeches, in which the words "translucence" and "opacity" rose and burst like bubbles, now sounded in Cincinnatus's ears, and the rush of blood became applause, and Marthe's locket-like face remained in his field of vision and faded only when the judge—who had moved so close that on his large swarthy nose he could see the enlarged pores, one of which, on the very extremity, had sprouted a lone but long hair—pronounced in a moist undertone, "with the gracious consent of the audience, you will be made to don the red tophat"—a token phrase that the courts had evolved, whose true meaning was known to every schoolboy.

"And yet I have been fashioned so painstakingly," thought Cincinnatus as he wept in the darkness. "The curvature of my spine has been calculated so well, so mysteriously. I feel, tightly rolled up in my calves, so many miles that I could yet run in my lifetime. My head is so comfortable . . ."

The clock struck a half, pertaining to some unknown hour.

Two

The morning papers, brought to him with a cup of tepid chocolate by Rodion, the local sheet *Good Morning Folks,* and the more serious daily *Voice of the Public,* teemed as always with color photographs. In the first one he found the façade of his house: the children looking out from the balcony, his father-in-law looking out of the kitchen window, a photographer looking out of Marthe's window; in the second one there was the familiar view from this window, looking out on the garden, showing the apple tree, the open gate and the figure of the photographer shooting the façade. In addition he found two snapshots of himself, depicting him in his meek youth.

Cincinnatus was the son of an unknown transient and

spent his childhood in a large institution beyond the Strop River (only in his twenties did he casually meet twittering, tiny, still so young-looking Cecilia C., who had conceived him one night at the Ponds when she was still in her teens). From his earliest years Cincinnatus, by some strange and happy chance comprehending his danger, carefully managed to conceal a certain peculiarity. He was impervious to the rays of others, and therefore produced when off his guard a bizarre impression, as of a lone dark obstacle in this world of souls transparent to one another; he learned however to feign translucence, employing a complex system of optical illusions, as it were—but he had only to forget himself, to allow a momentary lapse in self control, in the manipulation of cunningly illuminated facets and angles at which he turned his soul, and immediately there was alarm. In the midst of the excitement of a game his coevals would suddenly forsake him, as if they had sensed that his lucid gaze and the azure of his temples were but a crafty deception and that actually Cincinnatus was opaque. Sometimes, in the midst of a sudden silence, the teacher, in chagrined perplexity, would gather up all the reserves of skin around his eyes, gaze at him for a long while, and finally say: "What is wrong with you, Cincinnatus?" Then Cincinnatus would take hold of himself, and, clutching his own self to his breast, would remove that self to a safe place.

In the course of time the safe places became ever fewer: the solicitous sunshine of public concern penetrated everywhere, and the peephole in the door was placed in such a way that in the whole cell there was not a single point that the observer on the other side of the door could not pierce with his gaze. Therefore Cincinnatus did not crumple the motley newspapers, did not hurl them, as his double did (the double, the gangrel, that accompanies each of us —you, and me, and him over there—doing what we would like to do at that very moment, but cannot . . .). Cincinnatus very calmly laid the papers aside and finished his chocolate. The brown skim that had mantled the chocolate became shriveled scum on his lips. Then Cincinnatus put on the black dressing gown (which was too long for him), the black slippers with pompons, and the black skullcap, and began walking about the cell, as he had done every morning since the first day of his confinement.

Childhood on suburban lawns. They played ball, pig, daddy-longlegs, leapfrog, rumpberry, poke. He was light and nimble, but they did not like to play with him. In winter the city slopes were covered with a smooth sheet of snow, and what fun it was to hurtle down on the so-called "glassy" Saburov sleds. How quickly night would fall, when one was going home after sledding . . . What stars, what thought and sadness up above, and what ignorance below. In the frosty metallic dark the edible windows glowed with amber and crimson light; women in fox furs over silk dresses ran across the street from house to house; the electric "wagonet" stirred up a momentary luminescent blizzard as it sped by over the snow-powdered track.

A small voice: "Arkady Ilyich, take a look at Cincinnatus . . ."

He was not angry at the informers, but the latter multiplied and, as they matured, became frightening. Cincinnatus, who seemed pitch-black to them, as though he had been cut out of a cord-size block of night, opaque Cincinnatus would turn this way and that, trying to catch the rays, trying with desperate haste to stand in such a way as to seem translucent. Those around him understood each other at the first word, since they had no words that would end in an unexpected way, perhaps in some archaic letter, an upsilamba, becoming a bird or a catapult with wondrous consequences. In the dusty little museum on Second Boulevard, where they used to take him as a child, and where he himself would later take his charges, there was a collection of rare, marvelous objects, but all the townsmen except Cincinnatus found them just as limited and transparent as they did each other. *That which does not have a name does not exist.* Unfortunately everything had a name.

"Nameless existence, intangible substance," Cincinnatus read on the wall where the door covered it when open.

"Perpetual name-day celebrants, you can just..." was written in another place.

Further to the left, in a strong and neat hand, without a single superfluous line: "Note that when they address you..." The continuation had been erased.

Next to this, in clumsy childish letters: "I will collect fines from writers," signed "director of the prison."

One could make out yet another line, an ancient and enigmatic one: "Measure me while I live—after it will be too late."

"In any case I have been measured," said Cincinnatus, resuming his journey and rapping lightly with his knuckles on the walls. "But how I don't want to die! My soul has burrowed under the pillow. Oh, I don't want to! It will be cold getting out of my warm body. I don't want to... wait a while... let me doze some more."

Twelve, thirteen, fourteen. At fifteen Cincinnatus went
to work in the toy workshop, where he was assigned by
reason of his small stature. In the evenings he would feast
on ancient books to the lazy enchanting lap of wavelets in
the Floating Library, in memoriam of Dr. Sineokov, who
had drowned at just that spot in the city river. The grind-
ing of chains, the little gallery with its orange-colored lamp
shades, the plash, the water's smooth surface oiled by the
moon, and, in the distance, lights flickering past in the
black web of a lofty bridge. Later, however, the valuable
volumes began to suffer from the damp, so that in the end
it was necessary to drain the river, channeling all the water
over to the Strop by means of a specially dug canal.

In the shop he struggled for a long time with intricate
trifles and worked on rag dolls for schoolgirls; here there
was little hairy Pushkin in a fur carrick, and ratlike Gogol
in a flamboyant waistcoat, and old little Tolstoy with his
fat nose, in a peasant's smock, and many others, as for example Dobrolyubov, in spectacles without lenses and all
buttoned up. Having artificially developed a fondness for
this mythical Nineteenth Century, Cincinnatus was ready
to become completely engrossed in the mists of that antiquity and find therein a false shelter, but something else
distracted him.

There, in that little factory, worked Marthe; her moist
lips half open, aiming a thread at the eye of a needle.
"Hi, Cincinnatik!" And so began those rapturous wander-
ings in the very, very spacious (so much so that even the
hills in the distance would be hazy from the ecstasy of
their remoteness) Tamara Gardens, where, for no reason,
the willows weep into three brooks, and the brooks, in three

cascades, each with its own small rainbow, tumble into the lake, where a swan floats arm in arm with its reflection. The level lawns, the rhododendrons, the oak groves, the merry gardeners in their green jackboots playing hide-and-seek the whole day through; some grotto, some idyllic bench, on which three jokers had left three neat little heaps (it's a trick—they are imitations made of brown painted tin), some baby deer, bounding into the avenue and before your very eyes turning into trembling mottles of sunlight— that is what those gardens were like! There, there is Marthe's lisping prattle, her white stockings and velvet slippers, her cool breast and her rosy kisses tasting of wild strawberries. If only one could see from here—at least the treetops, at least the distant range of hills . . . Cincinnatus tied the dressing gown a little tighter. Cincinnatus moved the table and began dragging it backwards as it shrieked with rage: how unwillingly, with what shudderings it moved across the stone floor! Its shudderings were transmitted to Cincinnatus's fingers and to Cincinnatus's palate as he retreated toward the window (that is, toward the wall where way, way up high, there was the inclined cavity of the window). A loud spoon fell, the cup began to dance, the pencil started to roll, one book began sliding upon another. Cincinnatus lifted the bucking chair onto the table. Finally he climbed up himself. But of course he could see nothing, only the hot sky with a few white hairs thinly combed back —the remnants of clouds that could not tolerate the blueness. Cincinnatus could barely stretch as far as the bars beyond which rose the window tunnel with more bars at the end, and their shadowed repetition on the peeling walls of the stone incline. There, on the side, written in the same neat, contemptuous hand as one of the half-erased sentences he had read before, was the inscription: "You cannot see anything. I tried it too."

Cincinnatus was standing on tiptoe, holding the iron bars with his small hands, which were all white from the strain, and half of his face was covered with a sunny grating, and the gold of his left mustache shone, and there was a tiny golden cage in each of his mirrorlike pupils, while below, from behind, his heels rose out of the too-large slippers.

"A little more and you'll have a fall," said Rodion, who had been standing nearby for a full half minute and now firmly clenched the leg of the trembling chair. "It's all right, it's all right. You can climb down now."

Rodion had cornflower-blue eyes and, as always, his splendid red beard. This attractive Russian countenance was turned upwards toward Cincinnatus, who stepped on it with his naked sole—that is, his double stepped on it, while Cincinnatus himself had already descended from the chair to the table. Rodion, embracing him like a baby, carefully took him down, after which he moved the table with a violinlike sound to its previous place and sat on the edge, dangling the foot that was in the air, and bracing the other against the floor, having assumed the imitation-jaunty pose of operatic rakes in the tavern scene, while Cincinnatus picked at the sash of his dressing gown, and did his best not to cry.

Rodion was singing in his bass-baritone, rolling his eyes, brandishing the empty mug. Marthe used to sing that same dashing song once. Tears gushed from the eyes of Cincinnatus. On a climactic note Rodion sent the mug crashing against the floor and slid off the table. His song went on in chorus, even though he was alone. Suddenly he raised both arms and went out.

Sitting on the floor, Cincinnatus looked upward through his tears; the shadow of the bars had already moved. He tried—for the hundredth time—to move the table, but, alas, the legs had been bolted down for ages. He ate a pressed fig and began again to walk about the cell.

Nineteen, twenty, twenty-one. At twenty-two he was transferred to a kindergarten as a teacher in division F, and at that time he married Marthe. Almost immediately after he had assumed his new duties (consisting of keeping busy little children who were lame, hunchbacked or crosseyed) an important personage made a second-degree complaint against him. Cautiously, in the form of a conjecture, there was expressed the suggestion of Cincinnatus's basic illegality. Together with this memorandum the city fathers also examined the old complaints that had been made from time to time by the more perceptive of his colleagues at the workshop. The chairman of the education committee and certain other official figures took turns locking themselves up with him and making on him the tests prescribed by law. For several days in a row he was not allowed to sleep, and was compelled to keep up rapid senseless small talk until it bordered on delirium, to write letters to various objects and natural phenomena, enact everyday scenes, and to imitate various animals, trades and maladies. All of this he performed, all of this he passed, because he was young, resourceful, fresh, yearning to live, to live for a while with Marthe. Reluctantly they released him, allowing him to continue working with children of the lowest category, who were expendable, in order to see what would come of it.

He took them for walks, in pairs, while he turned the handle of a small portable music box that looked like a coffee grinder; on holidays he would swing with them at the playground—the whole cluster would be still and breathless as it soared and would squeal as it plummeted down. Some of them he taught to read.

Meanwhile Marthe began deceiving him during the very first year of their marriage; anywhere and with anybody. Generally when Cincinnatus came home she would have a certain sated half-smile on her face as she pressed her plump chin against her neck, as if reproaching herself, and, gazing up with her honest hazel eyes, would say in a soft cooing voice, "Little Marthe did it again today." He would look at her for a few seconds, pressing his palm to his cheek like a woman, and then, whining soundlessly, would go off through all the rooms full of her relatives and lock himself in the bathroom, where he would stamp his feet, let the water run and cough so as to cover up the sound of his weeping. Sometimes, to justify herself, she would explain to him, "You know what a kind creature I am: it's such a small thing, and it's such a relief to a man."

Soon she became pregnant, and not by him. She bore a boy, immediately got pregnant again—again not by him— and bore a girl. The boy was lame and evil-tempered, the girl dull, obese and nearly blind. Because of their defects both children ended up in his kindergarten, and it was odd to see nimble, sleek, rosy Marthe leading home this cripple and this stocky tot. Gradually Cincinnatus stopped watching himself altogether, and one day, at some open meeting in the city park there was a sudden wave of alarm and someone said in a loud voice, "Citizens, there is among us a ———" Here followed a strange, almost forgotten word, and the wind swished through the locust trees, and Cincinnatus found nothing better than to get up and walk away, absent-mindedly picking leaves from bushes bordering the path. And ten days later he was arrested.

"Tomorrow, probably," said Cincinnatus as he slowly walked about the cell. "Tomorrow, probably," said Cincinnatus and sat down on the cot, kneading his forehead with the palm of his hand. A sunset ray was repeating effects that were already familiar. "Tomorrow, probably," said Cincinnatus with a sigh. "It was too quiet today, so tomorrow, bright and early . . ."

For a while they were all silent—the earthenware pitcher with water at the bottom that had offered drink to all the prisoners of the world; the walls, with their arms around each other's shoulders like a foursome discussing a square secret in inaudible whispers; the velvet spider, somehow resembling Marthe; the large black books on the table . . .

"What a misunderstanding" said Cincinnatus and suddenly burst out laughing. He stood up and took off the dressing gown, the skullcap, the slippers. He took off the linen trousers and shirt. He took off his head like a toupee, took off his collarbones like shoulder straps, took off his rib cage like a hauberk. He took off his hips and his legs, he took off his arms like gauntlets and threw them in a corner. What was left of him gradually dissolved, hardly coloring the air. At first Cincinnatus simply reveled in the coolness; then, fully immersed in his secret medium, he began freely and happily to . . .

The iron thunderclap of the bolt resounded, and Cincinnatus instantly grew all that he had cast off, the skullcap included. Rodion the jailer brought a dozen yellow plums in a round basket lined with grape leaves, a present from the director's wife.

Cincinnatus, your criminal exercise has refreshed you.

Three

       Cincinnatus was awakened by the doomlike din of voices mounting in the corridor.

Even though the day before he had prepared for such an awakening, still he could not cope with his breathing and the beating of his heart. Folding the dressing gown over his heart so that it would not see—be quiet, it is nothing (as one says to a child at the moment of an incredible disaster)— covering his heart and raising himself slightly, Cincinnatus listened. There was the shuffling of many feet, at various levels of audibility; there were voices, also at various depths; one surged up, with a question; another, closer, responded. Hastening from afar, someone whizzed by and started to slide over the stone as over ice. In the midst of the hubbub the director's bass uttered several words, indistinct but definitely imperative. The most frightening thing was that all this bustle was pierced by a child's voice—the director had a small daughter. Cincinnatus distinguished both the whining tenor of his lawyer and the muttering of Rodion ... And again somebody on the run asked a booming question, and somebody boomingly answered. A huffing, a crackling, a clattering, as if someone were probing with a stick under a bench. "Couldn't find it?" the director inquired distinctly. Footsteps ran past. Footsteps ran past. Ran past and returned. Cincinnatus could not bear it any longer; he lowered his feet to the floor: they had not let him see Marthe after all. ... Should I begin dressing, or will they come to costume me? Oh, have done with it, come in ...

However, they tortured him for another two minutes or so. Suddenly the door opened, and, gliding, his lawyer rushed in.

He was ruffled and sweaty. He was fiddling with his left cuff and his eyes were wandering around.

"I lost a cuff link," he exclaimed, panting rapidly like a dog. "Must have—rushed against some—when I was with sweet little Emmie—she's always so full of mischief—by the coattails—everytime I drop in—and the point is that I heard something—but I didn't pay any—look, the chain must have—I was very fond of—well, it's too late now—maybe I can still—I promised all the guards—it's a pity, though—"

"A foolish, sleepy error," said Cincinnatus quietly. "I misinterpreted the fuss. This sort of thing is not good for the heart."

"Oh, thanks, don't worry about it, it's nothing," absent-mindedly muttered the lawyer. And with his eyes he literally scoured the corners of the cell. It was plain that he was upset by the loss of that precious object. It was plain. The loss of the object upset him. The object was precious. He was upset by the loss of the object.

With a soft groan Cincinnatus went back to bed. The other sat down at the foot of the cot.

"As I was coming to see you," said the lawyer, "I was so spry and cheerful ... But now this trifle has distressed me —for, after all, it is a trifle, you will agree; there are more important things. Well, how are you feeling?"

"In the mood for a confidential chat," replied Cincinnatus with eyes closed. "I want to share with you some conclusions I have reached. I am surrounded by some sort of wretched specters, not by people. They torment me as can torment only senseless visions, bad dreams, dregs of delirium, the drivel of nightmares and everything that passes down here for real life. In theory one would wish to wake up. But wake up I cannot without outside help, and yet I fear this help terribly, and my very soul has grown lazy and accustomed to its snug swaddling clothes. Of all the specters that surround me, you, Roman Vissarionovich, are probably the most wretched, but on the other hand—in view of your logical position in our invented habitus—you are in a manner of speaking, an adviser, a defender ..."

"At your service," said the lawyer, glad that Cincinnatus had at last become talkative.

"So this is what I want to ask you: on what grounds do they refuse to tell me the exact execution date? Wait a minute, I am not finished yet. The so-called director avoids a straight answer, and refers to the fact that—wait a minute!

I want to know, in the first place, who has the authority to appoint the day. I want to know, in the second place, how to get some sense out of that institution, or individual, or group of individuals . . ."

The lawyer, who had just been impatient to speak, now for some reason was silent. His made-up face with its dark blue eyebrows and long harelip revealed no particular mental activity.

"Leave your cuff alone," said Cincinnatus, "and try to concentrate."

Roman Vissarionovich jerkily changed the position of his body and clasped his restless fingers. In a plaintive voice he said, "It is exactly for that tone. . . ."

"That I am being executed," said Cincinnatus. "I know that. Go on!"

"Let's change the subject, I implore you," cried Roman Vissarionovich. "Can't you even now remain within legitimate limits? This is really awful. It is beyond my endurance. I dropped in merely to ask if you didn't have some legitimate wishes . . . for instance" (here his face lit up), "perhaps you should like to have printed copies of the speeches made at the trial? In case of such desire you must immediately submit the necessary petition, which you and I could prepare right now, with detailed specifications as to just how many copies of the speeches you require and for what purpose. I happen to have a free hour—Oh, please, please let's do this! I have even brought a special envelope."

"Just out of curiosity . . ." said Cincinnatus, "but first . . . Then, there is really no chance of getting an answer?"

"A special envelope," repeated the lawyer to tempt him.

"All right, let's have it," said Cincinnatus, and tore the thick, stuffed envelope into crimpy scraps.

"You shouldn't have done that," cried the lawyer, on the verge of tears. "You shouldn't have done that at all. You don't even realize what you have done. Perhaps there was a pardon in there. It won't be possible to get another!"

Cincinnatus picked up a handful of scraps and tried to reconstruct at least one coherent sentence, but everything was mixed up, distorted, disjointed.

"This is the sort of thing you always do," whined the lawyer, clutching his temples and pacing across the cell. "Perhaps your salvation was right in your very hands, and you ... It's horrible! Well, what shall I do with you? It's lost and gone now ... And I was so pleased! I was preparing you so carefully!"

"May I?" said the director in a distended voice as he opened the door ajar. "I shan't disturb you?"

"Please come in, Rodrig Ivanovich, please come in," said the lawyer. "Please come in, dear Rodrig Ivanovich. Only it is not very cheerful in here ..."

"Well, and how is our doomed friend today?" quipped the elegant, dignified director, compressing in his meaty purple paws the cold little hand of Cincinnatus. "Is every-thing all right? No aches or pains? Still gossiping with our indefatigable Roman Vissarionovich? Oh, by the way, dear Roman Vissarionovich, I have some good news for you— my little romp just found your cuff link on the stairs. *Là voici.* This is French gold, isn't it? Very, very dainty. I usually do not make compliments, but I must say. ..."

They both walked over to a corner, pretending to examine the charming trinket, discuss its history and value, marvel

at it. Cincinnatus took this opportunity to take up from
under the cot, and, with a high, purling sound, which became hesitant at the end, to . . .

"Yes, indeed, in excellent taste, excellent," the director
was repeating as he walked back from the corner with the
lawyer. "So you are feeling well, young man," he meaning-
lessly addressed Cincinnatus, who was climbing back into
bed. "However you must not be childish. The public, and
all of us, as representatives of the public, are interested only
in your welfare—that must be obvious by now. We are ready
to make things easier for you by relieving your loneliness.
In a few days a new prisoner will be moving in to one of
our deluxe cells. You will become acquainted, and that will
entertain you."

"In a few days?" asked Cincinnatus. "Then there *will* be
a few more days?"

"Listen to him," chuckled the director. "He has to know
everything. How do you like that, Roman Vissarionovich?"

"Oh, my friend, you are so right," sighed the lawyer.

"Yes, sir," continued the former, giving his keys a rattle.
"You ought to be more cooperative, mister. All the time he's
haughty, angry, snide. Last night I brought him some of
them plums, you know, and what do you think? His excellency did not choose to eat them, his excellency was too
proud. Yes sir! I started to tell you about that there new
prisoner. You will have your fill of chit-chat with him. No
need to mope as you do. Isn't that right, Roman Vissarionovich?"

"That's right, Rodion, that right," concurred the lawyer
with an involuntary smile.

Rodion stroked his beard and went on: "I've got to feeling

very sorry for the poor gentleman—I come in, I look, he's up on the table-and-chair, trying to reach the bars with his little hands and feet, like a sick monkey. And with the sky real blue, and the swallows a-flying, and cloudlets a-high— such bliss, such blessings! I take the gentleman down from the table like a baby, and meself I bawl—yes, just as I'm standing here—I bawl and bawl . . . I really went all to pieces, I was so sorry for him."

"Well, shall we take him upstairs, what do you think?" the lawyer suggested hesitantly.

"Why, sure thing, that we can," drawled Rodion with sedate benevolence. "We can always do that."

"Drape yourself in your dressing gown," uttered Roman Vissarionovich.

Cincinnatus said, "I obey you, specters, werewolves, parodies. I obey you. However, I demand—yes, demand" (and the other Cincinnatus began to stamp his feet hysterically, losing his slippers) "to be told how long I have left to live . . . and whether I shall be allowed to see my wife."

"You probably will," replied Roman Vissarionovich, after exchanging glances with Rodion. "Just don't you talk so much. All right, let's go."

"If you please," said Rodion, giving the unlocked door a shove with his shoulder.

All three went out: first Rodion, bowlegged, in old faded breeches, baggy in the seat; behind him the lawyer, in a frock coat, with a smudge on his celluloid collar and an edging of pinkish muslin at the back of his head where the black wig ended; and finally, behind him, Cincinnatus, losing his slippers, wrapping himself more tightly in his dressing gown.

At the bend in the corridor the other, nameless, guard gave them a salute. The pale stony light alternated with regions of darkness. They walked, and walked. One bend followed another. Several times they passed the very same design of dampness on the wall, looking like some dreadful ribby horse. Here and there it was necessary to turn on light; a dusty bulb, up above or at the side, would burst into bitter yellow light. Sometimes, also, it would be burned out, and then they would shuffle on through dense darkness. At one spot, where an unexpected and inexplicable sunbeam fell from above and glowed mistily as it broke on the eroded flagstones, Emmie, the director's daughter, in a bright checkered frock and checkered socks—a mere child, but with the marble calves of a little ballerina—was bouncing a ball, rhythmically against the wall. She turned, brushing a blond lock from her cheek with the fourth and fifth fingers of her hand, and followed the brief little procession with her eyes. Rodion gave a playful jingle with his keys as he passed; the lawyer lightly stroked her glowing hair; but she was staring at Cincinnatus, who gave her a frightened smile. Upon reaching the next bend of the passage, all three glanced back. Emmie was gazing after them, while she lightly plopped the glossy red and blue ball in her hands.

Again they walked in darkness for a long time, until they came to a dead end where a ruby bulb shone above a coiled fire hose. Rodion unlocked a low iron door; beyond it a stone staircase wound steeply upward. Here the order changed somewhat: Rodion marked time as he let first the lawyer and then Cincinnatus pass; upon which he softly fell in at the end of the procession.

It was not easy to climb the steep staircase, whose progress was accompanied by a gradual thinning of the gloom in which it grew, and they climbed for such a long time that, out of boredom, Cincinnatus began counting the steps, reached a three-digit number, but then stumbled and lost count. It grew lighter by degrees. Exhausted, Cincinnatus was climbing like a child, beginning with the same foot each time. One more twist, and suddenly there was a solid rush of wind, a dazzling expansion of summer sky, and the air was pierced by the cry of swallows.

Our travelers found themselves on a broad terrace at the top of a tower, whence there was a breathtaking view, since not only was the tower huge, but the whole fortress towered hugely on the crest of a huge cliff, of which it seemed to be a monstrous outgrowth. Far below one could see the almost vertical vineyards, and the creamy road that wound down to the dry river bed; a tiny person in red was crossing the convex bridge; the speck running in front of him was most likely a dog.

Further away the sun-flooded town described an ample hemicycle: some of the varicolored houses proceeded in even rows, accompanied by round trees, while others, awry, crept down slopes, stepping on their own shadows; one could distinguish the traffic moving on First Boulevard, and an amethystine shimmer at the end, where the famous fountain played; and still further, toward the hazy folds of the hills that formed the horizon, there was the dark stipple of oak groves, with, here and there, a pond gleaming like a hand mirror, while other bright ovals of water gathered, glowing through the tender mist, over there to the west, where the serpentine Strop had its source. Cincinnatus, his palm pressed to his cheek, in motionless, ineffably vague and perhaps even blissful despair, gazed at the glimmer and haze of the Tamara Gardens and at the dove-blue melting hills beyond them—oh, it was a long time before he could take his eyes away . . .

A few paces from him, the lawyer leaned his elbows on the broad stone parapet, whose top was overgrown with some kind of enterprising vegetable. His back was soiled with chalk. He peered pensively into space, his left patent-leather shoe placed upon his right, and so distending his cheeks with his fingers that his lower eyelids turned out. Rodion had found a broom somewhere and kept silent as he swept the terrace flagstones.

"How bewitching all this is," said Cincinnatus, addressing the gardens, the hills (and for some reason it was especially pleasant to repeat the word "bewitching" in the wind, somewhat as children cover and then expose their ears, amused at this renewal of the audible world). "Bewitching! I have never seen those hills look exactly like that, so mysterious. Somewhere among their folds, in their mysterious valleys, couldn't I . . . No, I had better not think about it."

He made a complete tour of the terrace. Flatlands stretched off to the north, with cloud shadows scudding across them; meadows alternated with grainfields. Beyond a bend of the Strop one could see the weed-blurred outlines of the ancient airport and the structure where they kept the venerable, decrepit airplane, with motley patches on its rusty wings, which was still sometimes used on holidays, principally for the amusement of cripples. Matter was weary. Time gently dozed. There was in town a certain man, a pharmacist, whose great-grandfather, it was said, had left a memoir describing how merchants used to go to China by air.

Cincinnatus completed his trip around the terrace and returned to its south parapet. His eyes were making highly illegal excursions. Now he thought he distinguished that very bush in flower, that bird, that path disappearing under a canopy of ivy—

"That will do now," said the director good-naturedly, tossing the broom in a corner and putting on again his frock coat. "Come along home."

"Yes, it's time," responded the lawyer, looking at his watch.

And the same little procession started back. In front was director Rodrig Ivanovich, behind him lawyer Roman Vissarionovich, and behind him prisoner Cincinnatus, who after so much fresh air was beset by spasms of yawning. The back of the director's frock coat was soiled with chalk.

Four

She came in, taking advantage of Rodion's morning visit, slipping beneath his hands, which were carrying the tray.

"Tut, tut, tut," said he, exorcising a storm of chocolate. With his soft foot he closed the door behind him, and muttered into his mustache, "What a naughty child . . ."

Meanwhile Emmie had hidden from him, squatting behind the table.

"Reading a book, eh?" observed Rodion, beaming with kindness. "That's a worthwhile pastime."

Without raising his eyes from the page Cincinnatus emitted an iambic assent, but his eyes no longer grasped the text.

45 ୧⋙

Rodion finished his uncomplicated duties, chased with a rag the dust dancing in a ray of sunlight, fed the spider, and left.

Emmie was still squatting, but a little less restrained, swaying a little as if on springs, her downy arms crossed, her pink mouth slightly open and her long, pale, almost white lashes nictating as she looked across the table-top at the door. An already familiar gesture: rapidly, with a haphazard selection of fingers, she brushed the flaxen hair from her temple, casting a sidelong glance at Cincinnatus, who had laid aside his book and was waiting to see what would come next.

"He is gone," said Cincinnatus.

She left her squatting position, but was still stooping and looking at the door. She was embarrassed and did not know what to undertake. Suddenly she showed her teeth and, with a flash of ballerina calves, flew to the door—which of course proved to be locked. Her moire sash quickened the air in the cell.

Cincinnatus asked her the usual two questions. Mincingly she gave her name and answered that she was twelve.

"And are you sorry for me?" asked Cincinnatus.

To this she made no answer. She raised up to her face the clay pitcher, which was standing in a corner. It was empty, hollow-sounding. She hoo-hooted into its depths a few times, and an instant later darted away; now she was leaning against the wall, supporting herself only with her shoulder blades and elbows, sliding forward on her tensed feet in their flat shoes, and straightening up again. She smiled to herself, and then, as she continued slithering, glanced at Cincinnatus with a slight scowl, as one looks at the low sun. All indications were that this was a wild, restless child.

"Aren't you just a little bit sorry for me?" said Cincinnatus. "It isn't possible. I cannot imagine it. Come on over here, you foolish little doe, and tell me on what day I shall die."

Emmie, however, made no reply, but slid down to the floor. There she quietly seated herself, pressing her chin against her bent knees, over which she stretched the hem of her skirt.

"Tell me, Emmie, please . . . Surely you know all about it—I can tell that you know . . . Your father has talked at the table, your mother has talked in the kitchen . . . Everybody is talking. Yesterday there was a neat little window cut out of the newspaper—that means people are discussing it, and I am the only one . . ."

As if caught in a whirlwind she jumped up from the floor, and, flying again to the door, began pounding on it, not with her palms, but, rather, with the heels of her hands. Her loose, silky-blond hair ended in hanging curls.

"If only you were grown up," mused Cincinnatus, "if your soul had a slight touch of my patina, you would, as in poetic antiquity, feed a potion to the turnkey, on a night that is murky. Emmie!" he exclaimed, "I implore you—and I shall not desist—tell me, when shall I die?"

Gnawing on a finger, she went over to the table, where the books towered in a pile. She flung one open, leafed through the pages, making them snap and almost ripping them out, banged it shut, picked up another. A rippling something kept running across her face: first she would wrinkle her freckled nose, then her tongue would distend her cheek from within.

The door clanged. Rodion, probably having looked through the peephole, came in, rather angry.

"Shoo, young lady! I'm the one who will catch it for this."

She broke into shrill laughter, dodged his crablike hand and rushed to the open door. There, on the threshold, she abruptly stopped with a dancer's magic precision and—perhaps blowing a kiss, or perhaps concluding a pact of silence—looked over her shoulder at Cincinnatus; whereupon, with the same rhythmic suddenness, she was off, running with long, high, springy steps, already preparing for flight.

Rodion, grumbling, jingling, trudged off after her.

"Wait a minute!" cried Cincinnatus. "I have finished all the books. Bring me again the catalogue."

"Books . . ." Rodion scoffed huffily and locked the door behind him with pronounced resonance.

What anguish! Cincinnatus, what anguish! What stone anguish, Cincinnatus—the merciless bong of the clock, and the obese spider, and the yellow walls, and the roughness of the black wool blanket. The skim on the chocolate. Pluck it with two fingers at the very center and snatch it whole from the surface, no longer a flat covering, but a wrinkled brown little skirt. The liquid is tepid underneath, sweetish and stagnant. Three slices of toast with tortoise shell burns. A round pat of butter embossed with the monogram of the director. What anguish, Cincinnatus, how many crumbs in the bed!

He lamented for a while, groaned, cracked all his joints, then he got up from the cot, put on the abhorred dressing gown, and began to wander around. Once again he examined all the inscriptions on the walls in the hope of somewhere discovering a new one. Like a fledgling crow on a stump, he stood for a long while on the chair, motionlessly gazing up at the beggarly ration of sky. He walked some more. Once more he read the eight rules for inmates, which he already knew by heart:

1. Leaving the prison building is positively forbidden.

2. A prisoner's meekness is a prison's pride.

3. You are firmly requested to maintain quiet between one and three P.M. daily.

4. You are not allowed to entertain females.

5. Singing, dancing and joking with the guards is permitted only by mutual consent and on certain days.

6. It is desirable that the inmate should not have at all, or if he does, should immediately himself suppress nocturnal dreams whose content might be incompatible with the condition and status of the prisoner, such as: resplendent landscapes, outings with friends, family dinners, as well as sexual intercourse with persons who in real life and in the waking state would not suffer said individual to come near, which individual will therefore be considered by the law to be guilty of rape.

7. Inasmuch as he enjoys the hospitality of the prison, the prisoner should in his turn not shirk participation in cleaning and other work of prison personnel in such measure as said participation is offered him.

8. The management shall in no case be responsible for the loss of property or of the inmate himself.

Anguish, anguish, Cincinnatus. Pace some more, Cincinnatus, brushing with your robe first the walls, then the chair. Anguish! The books heaped on the table have all been read. And, even though he knew that they had all been read, Cincinnatus searched, rummaged, peeked into a thick volume... Without sitting down, he leafed through the already familiar pages.

It was a bound magazine, published once upon a time, in a barely remembered age. The prison library, considered the second in the city for its size and the rarity of its volumes, kept several such curiosities. That was a remote world, where the simplest objects sparkled with youth and an inborn insolence, proceeding from the reverence that surrounded the labor devoted to their manufacture. Those were years of universal fluidity; well-oiled metals performed silent soundless acrobatics; the harmonious lines of men's suits were dictated by the unheard-of limberness of muscular bodies; the flowing glass of enormous windows curved around corners of buildings; a girl in a bathing suit flew like a swallow so high over a pool that it seemed no larger than a saucer; a high-jumper lay supine in the air, having already made such an extreme effort that, if it were not for the flaglike folds of his shorts, he would seem to be in lazy repose; and water ran, glided endlessly; the gracefulness of falling water, the dazzling details of bathrooms; the satiny ripples of the ocean with a two-winged shadow falling on it. Everything was lustrous and shimmering; everything gravitated passionately toward a kind of perfection whose definition was absence of friction. Reveling in all the temptations of the circle, life whirled to a state of such giddiness that the ground fell away and, stumbling, falling, weakened by nausea and languor—ought I to say it?—finding itself in a new dimension, as it were... Yes, matter has grown old

and weary, and little has survived of those legendary days—
a couple of machines, two or three fountains—and no one
regrets the past, and even the very concept of "past" has
changed.

"But then perhaps," thought Cincinnatus, "I am misinterpreting these pictures. Attributing to the epoch the char-
acteristics of its photograph. The wealth of shadows, the
torrents of light, the gloss of a tanned shoulder, the rare
reflection, the fluid transitions from one element to another
—perhaps all of this pertains only to the snapshot, to a
particular kind of heliotypy, to special forms of that art, and
the world really never was so sinuous, so humid and rapid—
just as today our unsophisticated cameras record in their
own way our hastily assembled and painted world."

"But then perhaps" (Cincinnatus began to write rapidly
on a sheet of ruled paper) "I am misinterpreting . . . Attributing to the epoch . . . This wealth . . . Torrents . . . Fluid
transitions . . . And the world really never was . . . Just as . . .
But how can these ruminations help my anguish? Oh, my
anguish—what shall I do with you, with myself? How dare
they conceal from me . . . I, who must pass through an ordeal of supreme pain, I, who, in order to preserve a semblance of dignity (anyway I shall not go beyond silent
pallor—I am no hero anyway . . .), must during that ordeal
keep control of all my faculties, I, I . . . am gradually weaken-
ing . . . the uncertainty is horrible—well, why don't you tell
me, do tell me—but no, you have me die anew every morning . . . On the other hand, were I to know, I could perform . . . a short work . . . a record of verified thoughts . . .
Some day someone would read it and would suddenly feel
just as if he had awakened for the first time in a strange

country. What I mean to say is that I would make him suddenly burst into tears of joy, his eyes would melt, and, after he experiences this, the world will seem to him cleaner, fresher. But how can I begin writing when I do not know whether I shall have time enough, and the torture comes when you say to yourself, 'Yesterday there would have been enough time'—and again you think, 'If only I had begun yesterday...' And instead of the clear and precise work that is needed, instead of a gradual preparation of the soul for that morning when it will have to get up, when—when you, soul, will be offered the executioner's pail to wash in— Instead, you involuntarily indulge in banal senseless dreams of escape—alas, of escape... Today, when she came running in, stamping and laughing—that is, I mean—No, I still ought to record, to leave something. I am not an ordinary —I am the one among you who is alive—Not only are my eyes different, and my hearing, and my sense of taste— not only is my sense of smell like a deer's, my sense of touch like a bat's—but, most important, I have the capacity to conjoin all of this in one point—No, the secret is not revealed yet—even this is but the flint—and I have not even begun to speak of the kindling, of the fire itself. My life. Once, when I was a child, on a distant school excursion, when I had got separated from the others—although I may have dreamt it—I found myself, under the sultry sun of midday, in a drowsy little town, so drowsy that when a man who had been dozing on a bench beneath a bright white-washed wall at last got up to help me find my way, his blue shadow on the wall did not immediately follow him. Oh, I know, I know, there must have been some oversight, on my part, and the shadow did not linger at all, but

simply, shall we say, it caught on the wall's unevenness ...
but here is what I want to express: between his movement
and the movement of the laggard shadow—that second,
that syncope—there is the rare kind of time in which I live
—the pause, the hiatus, when the heart is like a feather ...
And I would write also about the continual tremor—and
about how part of my thoughts is always crowding around
the invisible umbilical cord that joins this world to something—to what I shall not say yet ... But how can I write
about this when I am afraid of not having time to finish
and of stirring up all these thoughts in vain? When she
came rushing in today—only a child—here is what I want
to say—only a child, with certain loopholes for my thoughts
—I wondered, to the rhythm of an ancient poem—could she
not give the guards a drugged potion, could she not rescue
me? If only she would remain the child she is, but at the
same time mature and understand—and then it would be
feasible: her burning cheeks, a black windy night, salvation, salvation ... And I'm wrong when I keep repeating
that there is no refuge in the world for me. There is! I'll
find it! A lush ravine in the desert! A patch of snow in the
shadow of an alpine crag! This is unhealthy, though—what
I am doing: as it is I am weak, and here I am exciting myself, squandering the last of my strength. What anguish,
oh, what anguish ... And it is obvious to me that I have
not yet removed the final film from my fear."

He became lost in thought. Then he dropped the pencil,
got up, began walking. The striking of the clock reached his
ears. Using its chimes as a platform, footfalls rose to the
surface; the platform floated away, but the footfalls re-

mained and now two persons entered the cell: Rodion with
the soup and the Librarian with the catalogue.

The latter was a man of tremendous size but sickly appearance, pale, with shadows under his eyes, with a bald
spot encircled by a dark crown of hair, with a long torso
in a blue sweater, faded in places and with indigo patches
on the elbows. He had his hands in the pockets of his pants,
which were narrow as death, and clutched under his arm a
large book, bound in black leather. Cincinnatus had already
once had the pleasure of seeing him.

"The catalogue," said the Librarian, whose speech was
distinguished by a kind of defiant laconicism.

"Fine, leave it here," said Cincinnatus, "I shall choose
something. If you would like to wait, to sit down for a
minute, please do. If, however, you should like to go ..."

"To go," said the Librarian.

"All right. Then I shall return the catalogue through
Rodion. Here, you may take these back with you ... These
magazines of the ancients are wonderfully moving ... With
this weighty volume I went down, you know, as with a
ballast, to the bottom of time. An enchanting sensation."

"No," said the Librarian.

"Bring me some more—I'll copy out the years I want.
And some novel, a recent one. You are going already? You
have everything?"

Left alone, Cincinnatus went to work on the soup, simultaneously leafing through the catalogue. Its nucleus was
carefully and attractively printed; amid the printed text
numerous titles were inserted in red ink, in a small but precise hand. It was difficult for someone who was not a
specialist to make sense of the catalogue, since the titles

were arranged not in alphabetical order, but according to the number of pages in each, with notations as to how many extra sheets (in order to avoid duplication) had been pasted into this or that book. Therefore Cincinnatus searched without any definite goal in mind, picking out whatever happened to seem attractive. The catalogue was kept in a state of exemplary cleanness; this made it all the more surprising that on the white verso of one of the first pages a child's hand had made a series of pencil drawings, whose meaning at first escaped Cincinnatus.

Five

"Please accept my sincerest congratulations," said the director in his unctuous bass as he entered Cincinnatus's cell next morning. Rodrig Ivanovich seemed even more spruce than usual: the dorsal part of his best frock coat was stuffed with cotton padding like a Russian coachman's, making his back look broad, smooth, and fat; his wig was glossy as new; the rich dough of his chin seemed to be powdered with flour, while in his buttonhole there was a pink waxy flower with a speckled mouth. From behind his stately figure—he had stopped on the threshold— the prison employees peeked curiously, also decked out in their Sunday best, also with their hair slicked down; Rodion had even put on some little medal.

"I am ready. I shall get dressed at once. I knew it would be today."

"Congratulations," repeated the director, paying no attention to Cincinnatus's jerky agitation. "I have the honor to inform you that henceforth you have a neighbor—yes, yes, he has just moved in. You have grown tired of waiting, I bet? Well, don't worry—now, with a confidant, with a pal, to play and work with, you won't find it so dull. And, what is more—but this, of course, must remain strictly between ourselves—I can inform you that permission has come for you to have an interview with your spouse, *demain matin.*"

Cincinnatus lay back down on the cot and said, "Yes, that's fine. I thank you, rag doll, coachman, painted swine ... Excuse me, I am a little ..."

Here the walls of the cell started to bulge and dimple, like reflections in disturbed water; the director began to ripple, the cot became a boat. Cincinnatus grabbed the side in order to keep his balance, but the oarlock came off in his hand, and, neck-deep, among a thousand speckled flowers, he began to swim, got tangled, began sinking. Sleeves rolled up, they started poking at him with punting poles and grappling hooks, in order to snare him and pull him to the shore. They fished him out.

"Nerves, nerves, a regular little woman," said the prison doctor—alias Rodrig Ivanovich—with a smile. "Breathe freely. You can eat everything. Do you ever have night sweats? Go on as you are, and, if you are very obedient, maybe we shall let you take a quick peek at the new boy ... but mind you, only a quick peek ..."

"How long ... that interview ... how much time shall we be given? ..." Cincinnatus uttered with difficulty.

"In a minute, in a minute. Do not be in such a hurry, do not get excited. We promised to show him to you, and we will. Put on your slippers, straighten your hair. I think that . . ." The director looked interrogatively at Rodion, who nodded. "But please observe absolute silence," he again addressed Cincinnatus, "and don't grab at anything with your hands. Come, get up, get up. You haven't deserved this—you, my friend, are behaving badly, but still you have the permission—Now—not a word, quiet as a mouse . . ."

On tiptoe, balancing with his arms, Rodrig Ivanovich left the cell and with him went Cincinnatus in his oversize shuffling slippers. In the depths of the corridor Rodion was already stooping at a door with imposing bolts: he had pushed aside the cover of the peephole and was peering into it. Without turning, he made a motion with his hand demanding even greater silence and then imperceptibly changed the gesture into a different, beckoning one. The director rose even higher on tiptoe and turned with a threatening grimace, but Cincinnatus could not help scraping a little with his feet. Here and there, in the semidarkness of the passageways, the shadowy figures of the prison employees gathered, stooped, shaded their eyes with their hands as if to make out something in the distance. Laboratory assistant Rodion let the boss look through the focused eyepiece. His back emitting a solid squeak, Rodrig Ivanovich bent to peer in . . . Meanwhile, in the gray shadows, indistinct figures noiselessly changed their positions, noiselessly summoned each other, formed ranks, and already their many silent feet were working in place like pistons, preparing to step out. At last the director slowly moved away and tugged Cincinnatus lightly by the sleeve, inviting him, as a professor would a layman who had dropped in, to examine the slide. Cincinnatus meekly placed his eye against the luminous circle. At first he saw only bubbles of sunlight and bands of color, but then he distinguished a cot, identical to the one he had in his cell; piled nearby were two good suitcases with gleaming locks and a large oblong case like the kind used to carry a trombone.

"Well, do you see anything?" whispered the director, stooping close to him, and reeking of lilies in an open grave. Cincinnatus nodded, even though he did not yet see the main attraction; he shifted his gaze to the left, and then really saw something.

Seated on a chair, sideways to the table, as still as if he were made of candy, was a beardless little fat man, about thirty years old, dressed in old-fashioned but clean and freshly ironed prison pajamas; he was all in stripes—in striped socks, and brand-new morocco slippers—and revealed a virgin sole as he sat with one stubby leg crossed over the other and clasped his shin with his plump hands; a limpid aquamarine sparkled on his auricular finger, his honey-blond hair was parted in the middle of his remarkably round head, his long eyelashes cast shadows on his cherubic cheek, and the whiteness of his wonderful, even teeth gleamed between his crimson lips. He seemed to be all frosted with gloss, melting just a little in the shaft of sunlight falling on him from above. There was nothing on the table except an elegant traveling clock encased in a leather case.

"That'll do now," whispered the director with a smile, "me want to looky too," and he again attached himself to the bright hole. Rodion indicated by signs to Cincinnatus that it was time to go home. The shadowy figures of the employees were respectfully approaching in single file: behind the director there was already a whole queue of people waiting to get a look; some had brought along their eldest sons.

"We certainly are spoiling you," muttered Rodion in conclusion, and for a long time was unable to unlock the door of Cincinnatus's cell, even honoring it with a potent bit of Russian swearing, which turned the trick.

Everything become quiet. Everything was the same as always.

"No, not everything—tomorrow you will come," Cincinnatus said aloud, still trembling from his recent swoon. "What shall I say to you," he continued thinking, murmuring, shuddering. "What will you say to me? In spite of everything I loved you, and will go on loving you—on my knees, with my shoulders drawn back, showing my heels to the headsman and straining my goose neck—even then. And afterwards—perhaps most of all *afterwards*—I shall love you, and one day we shall have a real, all-embracing explanation, and then perhaps we shall somehow fit together, you and I, and turn ourselves in such a way that we form one pattern, and solve the puzzle: draw a line from point A to point B . . . without looking, or, without lifting the pencil . . . or in some other way . . . we shall connect the points, draw the line, and you and I shall form that unique design for which I yearn. If they do this kind of thing to me every morning, they will get me trained and I shall become quite wooden."

Cincinnatus had a fit of yawning—the tears streamed down his cheeks, and still hump after hump swelled under his palate. It was nerves—he was not sleepy. He had to find something to keep him busy until tomorrow—fresh books had not yet arrived. He had not returned the catalogue yet . . . Oh yes, the little drawings! But now, in the light of tomorrow's interview . . .

A child's hand, undoubtedly Emmie's, had drawn a set of pictures, forming (as it had seemed to Cincinnatus yesterday) a coherent narrative, a promise, a sample of phantasy. First there was a horizontal line—that is, this stone floor; on it was a rudimentary chair somewhat like an insect, and above was a grating made of six squares. Then came the same picture but with the addition of a full moon, the corners of its mouth drooping sourly beyond the grating. Next, a stool composed of three strokes with an eyeless (hence, sleeping) jailer on it and, on the floor, a ring with six keys. Then the same key ring, only a little larger, with a hand, extremely pentadactyl and in a short sleeve, reaching for it. Here it begins to get interesting. The door is ajar in the next drawing, and beyond it something looking like a bird's spur—all that is visible of the fleeing prisoner. Then he himself, with commas on his head instead of hair, in a dark little robe, represented to the best of the artist's ability by an isosceles triangle; he is being led by a little girl: prong-like legs, wavy skirt, parallel lines of hair. Then the same again, only in the form of a plan: a square for the cell, an angled line for the corridor, with a dotted line indicating the route and an accordionlike staircase at the end. And finally the epilogue: the dark tower, above it a pleased moon, with the corners of its mouth curling upward.

No—this was only self-deception, nonsense. The child had doodled aimlessly . . . Let us copy out the titles and lay the catalogue aside. Yes, the child . . . With the tip of her tongue showing at the right corner of her mouth, tightly holding the stubby pencil, pressing down upon it with a finger white with effort . . . And then, after connecting a particularly successful line, leaning back, rolling her head this way and that, wriggling her shoulders, and, going back to work on the paper, shifting her tongue to the left corner . . . so painstakingly. . . . Nonsense, let's not dwell on it any more . . .

Trying to think of a way to enliven the listless hours, Cincinnatus decided to tidy up for tomorrow's Marthe. Rodion agreed to haul in another tub like the one in which Cincinnatus had splashed on the eve of the trial. While waiting for the water Cincinnatus sat down at the table; today the table was a little wobbly.

"The interview," wrote Cincinnatus, "signifies, in all probability, that my terrible morning is already nearing. The day after tomorrow, at this very time, my cell will be empty. But I am happy that I shall see you. We used to go up to the workshops by two different staircases, the men by one, the women by the other, but would meet on the penultimate landing. No longer can I conjure Marthe as she was when I first met her, but I can recall having noticed at once that she opens her mouth a little an instant before laughing, and the round hazel eyes, and the coral earrings—oh, how I should like to reproduce her as she was, all new and still solid—and then the gradual softening—the fold between cheek and neck when she turned her head toward me, already grown warm, and almost alive. Her world. Her world consists of simple components, simply joined; I think that the simplest cook-book recipe is more complicated than the world that she bakes as she hums: every day for herself, for me, for everyone. But whence— even then, in the first days—whence the malice and obstinacy that suddenly... So soft, so amusing and warm, and then suddenly... At first I thought she was doing it deliberately, perhaps to show how another in her place might have grown shrewish and stubborn. Can you imagine my amazement when I realized that this was her real self! Because of what trifles—my foolish one, how little your head was, if one feels through all that auburn, thick mass to which she knows how to impart an innocent sleekness with a girlish gloss on the top of her head. 'Your little wife looks so quiet and gentle, but she bites, I tell you,' her first unforgettable lover said to me, and the base thing is that the verb was not being used figuratively... because it was true that at a certain moment... one of those memories that one should drive away, or else it will overpower and crush you. Little Marthe did it again.... And once I saw, I saw, I saw—from the balcony I saw—and since that day I would never enter any room without first announcing my approach from afar—by a cough, or a meaningless exclamation. How awful it was to glimpse that contortion, that breathless haste—all that had been mine in the shadowed seclusion of the Tamara Gardens, and that I had afterward

lost. Count how many she had ... endless torture: to talk
at dinner with one or another of her lovers, appear cheerful, crack nuts, crack jokes, and all the while to be mortally
afraid to bend down, and chance to see the nether half of
that monster whose upper half was quite presentable, having the appearance of a young woman and a young man
visible down to the waist at table, peacefully feeding and
chatting; and whose nether half was a writhing, raging
quadruped. I descended into hell to retrieve a dropped
napkin. Later Marthe would say of herself (in that same
first person plural), 'We are very much ashamed that we
were seen,' and pouted. And still I love you. Inescapably,
fatally, incurably ... As long as the oaks stand in those
gardens, I will ... When they gave you official proof that I
was not wanted, that I was to be shunned—you were surprised that you had noticed nothing yourself—and yet it
was so easy to hide it from you! I remember how you implored me to reform, with no real understanding what it
was in me that ought to be reformed and how one would
go about it, and even now you do not understand anything,
do not for a moment stop to think whether you understand
or not, and, when you wonder, your wonder is almost cozy.
Still, when the bailiff began going around the courtroom
with the hat, you too threw in your scrap of paper."

As the tub rocked at the wharf, an innocent, gay, inviting steam rose above it. Impulsively, in two quick motions,
Cincinnatus heaved a sigh and laid aside the filled sheets.
From his modest footlocker he produced a clean towel.
Cincinnatus was so small and slender that he was able to
get all of himself into the washing tub. He sat there as in
a canoe and floated peacefully. A reddish evening ray, min-

gling with the steam, aroused a motley tremor in the small
world of the stone cell. Reaching shore, Cincinnatus stood
up and stepped out onto land. As he dried himself he
struggled with dizziness and palpitations. He was very thin,
and now, as the light of the setting sun exaggerated the
shadows of his ribs, the very structure of his rib cage seemed
a triumph of cryptic coloration inasmuch as it expressed
the barred nature of his surroundings, of his gaol. My poor
little Cincinnatus. As he dried himself, trying to find some
diversion in his own body, he kept examining his veins and
he could not help thinking how he would soon be uncorked,
and all the contents would run out. His bones were light
and thin; his meek toe nails (you dear ones, you innocent
ones) gazed up at him with childlike attention; and, as he
sat thus on the cot—naked, his entire skinny back, from
coccyx to cervical vertebrae, exposed, to the observers on
the other side of the door (he could hear whispers, rustling
movements, a discussion of something or other—but never
mind, let them look), Cincinnatus might have passed for
a sickly youth—even the back of his head, with its hollowed
nape and tuft of wet hair, was boyish—and exceptionally
handy. From the same valise Cincinnatus took a small mirror
and a vial of depilatory water which always reminded him
of that marvelously hirsute mole which Marthe had on her
side. He rubbed it into his prickly cheeks, removing the
prickliness and carefully avoiding the mustache.

Nice and clean now. He heaved a sigh and put on the
cool nightshirt, still smelling of home washing.

It grew dark. He lay in bed and kept floating. At the customary hour Rodion turned on the light and removed the

bucket and the tub. The spider lowered itself to him on a thread and settled on the finger which Rodion offered to the furry beastie, chatting with it as with a canary. Meanwhile the door to the corridor remained ajar, and all at once something stirred there ... for an instant the twining tips of pale curls drooped, and then disappeared when Rodion moved as he gazed up at the tiny black aerialist receding up under the circus dome. The door still remained a quarter of the way open. Heavy Rodion, with his leather apron and his crinky red beard, lumbered about the cell, and, when the clock (closer now because of the direct communication) began its hoarse rattle prior to striking, he produced a thick watch from a recess in his belt and checked the time. Then, supposing Cincinnatus to be asleep, he watched him for a rather long time, leaning on his broom as on a halberd. Having reached who knows what conclusions he moved again ... Just then, silently and not very fast, a red-and-blue ball rolled in through the door, followed one leg of a right triangle straight under the cot, disappeared for an instant, thumped against the chamber pot, and rolled out along the other cathetus—that is, toward Rodion, who all without noticing it, happened to kick it as he took a step; then, following the hypotenuse, the ball departed into the same chink through which it had entered. Shouldering the broom, Rodion left the cell. The light went out.

Cincinnatus did not sleep, did not sleep, did not sleep— no, he was asleep, but with a moan scrambled out again— and now again he did not sleep, slept, did not sleep, and everything was jumbled—

Marthe, the executioner's block, her velvet—and how will

it turn out...which will it be? A beheading or a tryst? Everything merged totally, but he did open his eyes for just one more wink when the light went on and Rodion entered on tiptoe, took the catalogue in its black binding from the table, went out, and it became dark.

Six

What was it—through everything terrible, nocturnal, unwieldy—what was that thing? It had been last to move aside, reluctantly yielding to the huge, heavy wagons of sleep, and now it was first to hurry back—so pleasant, so very pleasant—swelling, growing more distinct, suffusing his heart with warmth: Marthe is coming today!

Just then Rodion brought a lilac letter on a salver as they do in plays. Cincinnatus perched on the bed and read the following: "A million apologies! An inexcusable blunder! Upon consulting the text of the law it was discovered that an interview is granted only upon expiration of one week following the trial. Hence we shall postpone it until to-morrow. Best of health, old boy, regards. Everything the same here, one worry after another, the paint sent for the sentry boxes again turned out to be worthless, about which I had already written, but without results."

Rodion, trying not to look at Cincinnatus, was gathering yesterday's dishes from the table. It must be a dreary day: the light penetrating from above was gray, and compassionate Rodion's dark leather clothes seemed damp and stiff.

"Oh well," said Cincinnatus, "as you wish, as you wish . . . I am powerless anyway." (The other Cincinnatus . . . a little smaller, was crying, all curled up in a ball.) "All right, let it be tomorrow. But I should like to ask you to call . . ."

"Right away," blurted out Rodion with such alacrity that he seemed to have been longing just for this; he was about to dash off but just then the director, who had been waiting too impatiently at the door, appeared just a split second too early, so that they collided.

Rodrig Ivanovich was holding a wall calendar and did not know where to lay it down.

"A million apologies," he cried, "an inexcusable blunder! Upon consulting the text of the law . . ." Having repeated his message verbatim Rodrig Ivanovich seated himself at Cincinnatus's feet and added hurriedly, "In any case you may submit a complaint, but I consider it my duty to warn you that the next congress will take place in the fall, and by then a lot of water—and not only water—will have flowed over the dam. Do I make myself clear?"

"I do not intend to complain," said Cincinnatus, "but wish to ask you, is there in the so-called order of so-called things of which your so-called world consists even one thing

that might be considered an assurance that you will keep
a promise?"

"A promise?" asked the director in surprise, ceasing to
fan himself with the cardboard part of the calendar (depicting the fortress at sunset, a water color). "What
promise?"

"That my wife will come tomorrow. So you will not agree
to guarantee it in this case—but I am phrasing my question
more broadly: is there in this world, can there be, any kind
of security at all, any pledge of anything, or is the very idea
of guarantee unknown here?"

A pause.

"Isn't it too bad though about Roman Vissarionovich,"
said the director, "have you heard? He is in bed with a cold,
and apparently quite a serious one . . ."

"I have a feeling that you will not answer me at any cost;
that is logical, for even irresponsibility in the end develops
its own logic. For thirty years I have lived among specters
that appear solid to the touch, concealing from them the
fact that I am alive and real—but now that I have been
caught, there is no reason to be constrained with you. At
least I shall test for myself all the unsubstantiality of this
world of yours."

The director cleared his throat and went on as if nothing
had happened: "So serious, in fact, that I as a doctor am
not certain whether he will be able to attend—that is,
whether he will recover in time—*bref*, whether he will be
able to make it to your show . . ."

"Go away," said Cincinnatus through clenched teeth.

"Do not be crestfallen," continued the director. "Tomorrow, tomorrow the thing you dream of will become a reality

... It's a cute calendar, though, isn't it? A work of art. No, this isn't for you."

Cincinnatus closed his eyes. When he opened them again, the director was standing in the center of the cell with his back toward him. The leather apron and red beard, apparently left behind by Rodion, were still cluttering the chair.

"Today we shall have to do a particularly good job of cleaning up your abode," he said without turning, "so as to prepare it for tomorrow's interview ... While we are washing the floor in here, I shall ask you to—"

Cincinnatus shut his eyes again, and the voice, grown smaller in volume, went on: "... I shall ask you to step out into the corridor. It will not take long. Let us make a real effort, so that tomorrow, in a fitting manner, neatly, smartly, festively ..."

"Get out," cried Cincinnatus, raising himself and shaking all over.

"Quite impossible," Rodion announced gravely, fussing with his apron straps. "We must do some work here. Just look at all the dust ... You'll say thankee yourself."

He inspected himself in a pocket mirror, fluffed up the whiskers on his cheeks and, at last approaching the cot, handed Cincinnatus his things. The slippers were providently stuffed with wadded paper, while the hem of the dressing gown was carefully folded back and pinned. Cincinnatus, a bit unsteady on his feet, got dressed and, leaning a little on the arm of Rodion, went out into the corridor. There he sat down on a stool, folding his arms into his sleeves like a sick man. Leaving the door of the ward wide open, Rodion began cleaning. The chair was placed atop the table; the sheet was stripped from the cot; the pail handle clinked; the draft riffled through the papers on the table, and one sheet glided to the floor. "What are you moping about there?" shouted Rodion, raising his voice above the noise of the water, the sloshing and clatter, "You ought to take a bit of a walk along the corridors there...Go on, don't be afraid—I'll be right here in case anything happens—all you have to do is holler."

Cincinnatus obediently rose from the stool, but barely had he moved along the cold wall—undoubtedly related to the rock on which the fortress had risen—barely had he walked a few steps away (and what steps!—feeble, weightless, meek), barely had he consigned Rodion, the open door, and the pails to a receding perspective, when Cincinnatus felt the surge of freedom. It flowed more fully when he turned the corner. Except for the sweaty smears and the cracks, the bare walls were adorned by nothing; only in one place someone had scrawled in ochre, with a house painter's stroke, "Testing brush, testing bru—" with an ugly run of paint under it. From the unaccustomed exertion of walking alone, Cincinnatus's muscles grew limp and there was a stitch in his side.

It was then that Cincinnatus stopped and, looking around him as if he had just entered this stony solitude, summoned up all his will, evoked the full extent of his life, and endeavored to comprehend his situation with the utmost exactitude. Accused of the most terrible of crimes, gnostical turpitude, so rare and so unutterable that it was necessary to use circumlocutions like "impenetrability," "opacity," "occlusion"; sentenced for that crime to death by beheading; emprisoned in the fortress in expectation of the unknown but near and inexorable date (which he distinctly anticipated as the wrenching, yanking and crunch of a monstrous tooth, his whole body being the inflamed gum, and his head that tooth); standing now in the prison corridor with a sinking heart—still alive, still unimpaired, still Cincinnatic—Cincinnatus C. felt a fierce longing for freedom, the most ordinary, physical, physically feasible kind of freedom, and instantly he imagined, with such sensuous clarity as though it all was a fluctuating corona emanating from him, the town beyond the shallowed river, the town, from every point of which one could see—now in this vista, now in that, now in crayon, and now in ink— the tall fortress within which he was. And so powerful and sweet was this tide of freedom that everything seemed better than it really was: his gaolers, who in fact were everyone, seemed more tractable; in the confining phenomena of life his reason sought out a possible trail, some kind of vision danced before his eyes—like a thousand iridescent needles of light that surround the dazzling reflection of the sun in a nickel-plated sphere ... Standing in the prison corridor and listening to the ample sonorities of the clock, which had just begun its leisurely enumeration, he imagined life in the city as it generally was at this fresh morning hour: Marthe, eyes lowered, is walking with an empty basket from the house along the blue sidewalk, followed at a distance of three paces by a dark-mustachioed young blade; the electric wagonets in the shape of swans or gondolas, where you sit as in a carrousel cradle, keep gliding in an endless stream along the boulevard; couches and armchairs are being carried out of furniture warehouses for airing, and passing school children sit down on them to rest, while the little orderly, his wheelbarrow loaded with all their books, mops his brow like a full-grown laborer; spring-powered, two-seat "clocklets," as they are called here in the provinces, click along over the freshly sprinkled pavement (and to think that these are the degenerate descendants of the machines of the past, of those splendid lacquered stream-lined automobiles . . . what made me think of that? ah yes, the photos in the magazine); Marthe picks out some fruit; decrepit, dreadful horses, which have long since ceased to marvel at the sights of hell, deliver merchandise from the factories to the city distributors; street bread vendors, white-shirted, with gilded faces, shout as they juggle their baton loaves, tossing them high in the air, catching them and twirling them once again; at a window overgrown with wisteria a gay foursome of telegraph workers are clinking glasses and drinking toasts to the health of passers-by; a famed punster, a gluttonous, coxcombed old man in red silk trousers, is gorging himself on fried chuckricks at a pavilion on the Lesser Ponds; the clouds disperse, and, to the accompaniment of a brass band, dappled sunlight runs along the sloping streets, and visits the side alleys; pedestrians walk briskly; the smell of lindens, of carburine and of damp gravel is in the air; the perpetual fountain at the mausoleum of Captain Somnus profusely irrigates with its spray the stone captain, the bas-relief at his elephantine feet and the quivering roses; Marthe, her eyes lowered, is walking homeward with a full basket, followed at a distance of three paces by a fair-haired fop . . . These are the things that Cincinnatus saw and heard through the walls as the clock struck, and, even though in reality everything in this city was always quite dead and awful by comparison with the secret life of Cincinnatus and his guilty flame, even though he knew this perfectly well and knew also that there was no hope, yet at this moment he still longed to be on those bright familiar streets ... but then the clock finished ringing, the imaginary sky grew overcast, and the jail was back in force.

Cincinnatus held his breath, moved, stopped again, listened: somewhere ahead, at an indeterminate distance, there was a tapping.

It was a rhythmic, quick, blunt sound, and Cincinnatus, all his nerves a-flutter, heard in it an invitation. He walked on, very attentive, very ethereal and lucid; he turned he knew not how many corners. The noise ceased, but then seemed to have flown nearer, like an invisible woodpecker. Tap, tap, tap. Cincinnatus quickened his pace, and once again the dark passage made a bend. Suddenly it became lighter—though still not like day—and now the noise became definite and almost smug. Ahead, in a flood of pale light, Emmie was bouncing a ball against the wall.

At this point the passage was wide, and at first it seemed to Cincinnatus that the left wall contained a large, deep window, through which all that strange additional light was flowing. Emmie, as she bent down to retrieve her ball, and at the same time to pull up her sock, looked at him slyly and shyly. The little blond hairs stood erect on her bare arms and shins. Her eyes shone between her whitish lashes. Now she straightened up, brushing the flaxen curls from her face with the same hand in which she was holding the ball.

"You aren't supposed to walk here," she said—she had something in her mouth; it rolled behind her cheek and knocked against her teeth.

"What is that you are sucking?" asked Cincinnatus.

Emmie stuck out her tongue; on its independently live tip lay a piece of brilliant barberry-red hard candy.

"I have some more," she said. "Want one?"

Cincinnatus shook his head.

"You aren't supposed to walk here," repeated Emmie.

"Why?" asked Cincinnatus.

She shrugged one shoulder and, grimacing, arching the hand in which she held the ball, tensing her calves, she went over to the spot where he had thought there was a niche, a window, and, fidgeting, suddenly seeming all legs, settled herself on a sill-like projection of stone.

No, it was only the semblance of a window; actually it was a glazed recess, a showcase, and it displayed in its false depth—yes, of course, how could one help but recognize it! —a view of the Tamara Gardens. This landscape, daubed in several layers of distance, executed in blurry green hues and illuminated by concealed bulbs, was reminiscent not so much of a terrarium or some model of theatrical scenery as of the backdrop in front of which a wind orchestra toils and puffs. Everything was reproduced fairly accurately as far as grouping and perspective was concerned, and, were it not for the drab colors, the stirless treetops and the torpid lighting, one could slit one's eyes and imagine oneself gazing through an embrasure, from this very prison, at those very gardens. The indulgent gaze recognized those avenues, that curly verdancy of groves, the portico at the right, the detached poplars, and, in the middle of the unconvincing blue of the lake, the pale blob that was probably a swan. Afar, in a stylized mist, the hills humped their round backs, and above them, in that kind of slate-blue firmament under which Thespians live and die, cumulus clouds stood still. And all of this was somehow not fresh, antiquated, covered with dust, and the glass through which Cincinnatus was looking bore smudges, from some of which a child's hand could be reconstructed.

"Won't you please take me out there?" whispered Cincinnatus. "I beseech you."

He was sitting next to Emmie on the stone projection and both of them were peering into the artificial remoteness beyond the glass; enigmatically, she kept following winding paths with her finger, and her hair smelled of vanilla.

"Pop's coming," she suddenly said in a husky, hurried voice; then she hopped to the floor and vanished.

It was true: Rodion was approaching, keys a-jangle, from the direction opposite the one whence Cincinnatus had come (who thought for a moment it was a reflection in a mirror).

"Home you go," he said jokingly.

The light behind the glass went out and Cincinnatus took a step, intending to return by the same route as he had come.

"Hey, hey, where are you off to?" exclaimed Rodion. "Go straight, it's shorter that way."

And only then did Cincinnatus realize that the bends in the corridor had not been leading him away anywhere, but rather formed a great polyhedron—for now, as he turned a corner, he saw his door in the distance, and, before he reached it, passed the cell where the new prisoner was kept. The door of this cell was wide open, and inside, the likable shorty whom he had seen before, dressed in his striped pajamas, was standing on a chair and tacking the calendar to the wall: tap, tap, like a woodpecker.

"No peeking, my fair damsel," said Rodion good-naturedly to Cincinnatus. "Home, home. And what a cleaning job we've done on your place, eh? Now we don't have to be ashamed about bringing guests in."

He seemed particularly proud of the fact that the spider was enthroned in a clean, impeccably correct web, which had been created, it was clear, just a moment before.

Seven

An enchanting morning! Freely, without the former friction, it penetrated through the barred glass washed yesterday by Rodion. Nothing could look more festive than the yellow paint of the walls. The table was covered by a clean tablecloth, which did not yet cling because of the air under it. The liberally doused stone floor exhaled fontal freshness.

Cincinnatus put on the best clothes he had with him— and while he was pulling on the white silk stockings which he, as a teacher, was entitled to wear at gala performances— Rodion brought in a wet cut-glass vase with jowly peonies from the director's garden and placed it on the table, in the center . . . no, not quite in the center; he backed out and in a minute returned with a stool and an additional chair, and arranged the furniture not haphazardly but with judgment and taste. He came back several times, and Cincinnatus did not dare ask, "will it be soon?" and—as happens at that particularly inactive hour when, all dressed up, you are awaiting guests—he strolled around, now perching in unaccustomed corners, now straightening the flowers in the vase, so that at last Rodion took pity on him and said it would not be long now.

Punctually at ten, Rodrig Ivanovich appeared, in his best, most monumental frock coat, pompous, aloof, excited yet composed; he set down a massive ash tray and inspected everything (with the exception only of Cincinnatus), acting like a major-domo engrossed in his job, who gives his attention to the neatness of the inanimate inventory only, leaving the animate to shift for themselves. He returned carrying a green flask equipped with a rubber bulb and began spraying pine fragrance, rather unceremoniously pushing aside Cincinnatus when the latter happened to get in his way. The chairs Rodrig Ivanovich arranged differently from Rodion, and for a long time he stared, goggle-eyed, at the backs, which did not match—one was lyrate, the other square. He puffed up his cheeks and let out the air with a whistle, and at last turned to Cincinnatus.

"And how about you? Are you ready?" he asked. "Did you find everything you needed? Are your shoe buckles in order? Why is it wrinkled, or something, over here? Shame on you—Let's see your paws. *Bon.* Now try not to get all dirty. I think it won't be long now . . ."

He went out, and his succulent, authoritative bass reverberated through the corridor. Rodion opened the cell door, securing it in that position, and unrolled a caramel-striped runner on the threshold. "Coming," he whispered with a wink and disappeared again. Now a key made a threefold clank in a lock somewhere, confused voices were audible, and a gust stirred the hair on Cincinnatus's head.

He was very agitated, and his quivering lips continuously assumed the shape of a smile. "Right this way. Here we are already," he could hear the sonorous comments of the director, and in the next instant the latter appeared, gallantly leading in by the elbow the plump, striped little prisoner who, before coming in, paused on the mat, noise-lessly brought together his morocco feet, and bowed grace-fully.

"Allow me to present to you M'sieur Pierre," said the director to Cincinnatus in jubilant tones. "Come in, come in, M'sieur Pierre. You can't imagine how you have been awaited here—Get acquainted, gentlemen—The long-awaited meeting—An instructive spectacle . . . Do bear with us, M'sieur Pierre, do not find fault . . ."

He did not even know what he was saying—he was bub-bling over, cutting heavy little capers, rubbing his hands, bursting with delighted embarrassment.

M'sieur Pierre, very calm and composed, walked in, bowed once again, and Cincinnatus mechanically joined him in a handshake; the other man retained Cincinnatus's escaping fingers in his small soft paw a second longer than is customary—as a gentle elderly doctor draws out a hand-shake, so gently, so appetizingly—and now he released it.

In a melodious, high-pitched voice coming from the throat M'sieur Pierre said, "I too am extremely happy to make your acquaintance at last. I make bold to hope that we may get to know each other more closely."

"Exactly, exactly," roared the director, "oh, please, be seated . . . Make yourself at home . . . Your colleague is so happy to see you here that he is at a loss for words."

M'sieur Pierre seated himself, and here it became evident that his legs did not quite reach the floor; however this did not detract in the least from his dignity or that particular grace with which nature endows a few select little fat men. His crystal-bright eyes gazed politely at Cincinnatus, while Rodrig Ivanovich, who had also sat down at the table, tittering, urging, intoxicated with pleasure, looked from one to the other, greedily following the impression made on Cincinnatus by the guest's every word.

M'sieur Pierre said: "You bear an extraordinary resemblance to your mother. I myself never had the chance of seeing her, but Rodrig Ivanovich kindly promised to show me her photograph."

"At your service," said the director, "we'll obtain one for you."

M'sieur Pierre continued: "Anyway, apart from this, I have been a photography enthusiast ever since I was young; I am thirty now, and you?"

"He is exactly thirty," said the director.

"You see, I guessed right. So, since this is your hobby too, let me show you—"

Briskly, he produced from the breast pocket of his pajama top a bulging wallet, and from it a thick batch of home snapshots of the smallest size. Riffling through them as through a deck of tiny cards, he began placing them one by one on the table, and Rodrig Ivanovich would grab each with delighted exclamations, examine it for a long time, and slowly, still admiring the snapshot, or else reaching for the next, would pass it on—even though all was still and silent there. The pictures showed M'sieur Pierre, M'sieur Pierre in various poses—now in a garden, with a giant prize tomato in his hand, now perching with one buttock on some railing (profile, with pipe), now reading in a rocking chair, a glass with a straw standing near him ...

"Excellent, marvelous," Rodrig Ivanovich would comment, fawning, shaking his head, feasting his eyes on every shot or else holding two at a time and shifting his gaze from one to the other. "My, my, what biceps you have in this one! Who would think—with your graceful physique. Overwhelming! Oh, how charming—talking with the little birdie!"

"A pet," said M'sieur Pierre.

"Most entertaining! What do you know ... And this here ... Eating a watermelon, no less!"

"Yep," said M'sieur Pierre. "You have already looked through those. Here are some more."

"Charming, let me tell you. Let's have that other batch— he hasn't seen them yet ..."

"Here I am juggling three apples," said M'sieur Pierre.

"Isn't that something!" said the director clucking his tongue.

"At breakfast," said M'sieur Pierre. "This is me, and that is my late father."

"Yes, yes, of course I recognize him ... That noble brow!"

"On the banks of the Strop," said M'sieur Pierre. "Have you been there?" he asked turning to Cincinnatus.

"I don't think he has," replied Rodrig Ivanovich. "And where was this taken? What an elegant little overcoat! You know something, you look older in this one. Just a second, I want to see that one again, with the watering can."

"There ... That is all I have with me," said M'sieur Pierre, and again addressed Cincinnatus: "If only I had known that you are so interested, I would have brought along more—I have a good dozen albums."

"Wonderful, stunning," repeated Rodrig Ivanovich, wiping with a lilac-colored handkerchief his eyes, grown moist from all these joyous titters and ejaculations.

M'sieur Pierre reassembled the contents of his wallet. Suddenly there was a deck of cards in his hands.

"Think of a card, please, any card," he proposed, laying the cards out on the table; he pushed the ash tray aside with his elbow; he continued laying.

"We have thought of one," said the director jauntily.

Indulging in a bit of hocus-pocus M'sieur Pierre put his index finger to his forehead; then he quickly gathered up the cards, smartly made the pack crackle and threw out a trey of spades.

"This is amazing," exclaimed the director. "Simply amazing!"

The deck vanished just as suddenly as it had appeared, and, making an imperturbable face, M'sieur Pierre said: "This little old woman comes to the doctor and says, 'I have a terrible malady, Mr. Doctor,' she says, 'I've an awful fright I'll die of it . . .' 'And what are the symptoms?' 'My head shakes, Mr. Doctor,' " and M'sieur Pierre, mumbling and shaking, imitated the little old woman.

Rodrig Ivanovich burst into riotous mirth, struck the table with his fist, nearly fell off his chair; then had a fit of coughing; moaned; and with a great effort regained control of himself.

"M'sieur Pierre, you are the life of the party," he said, still shedding tears, "truly the life of the party! I haven't heard such a hilarious anecdote in all my life!"

"How melancholy we are, how tender," said M'sieur Pierre to Cincinnatus, thrusting out his lips as if he were trying to make a sulking child laugh. "We keep so still, and our little mustache is all quivering, and the vein on our neck is throbbing, and our little eyes are misty . . ."

"It's all from joy," quickly inserted the director. "*N'y faites pas attention.*"

"Yes, it is indeed a happy day, a red-letter day," said M'sieur Pierre. "I am bubbling over with excitement myself . . . I don't want to boast, but in me, my dear colleague, you will find a rare combination of outward sociability and inward delicacy, the art of the causerie and the ability to keep silent, playfulness and seriousness . . . Who will console a sobbing infant, and glue his broken toy together? M'sieur Pierre. Who will intercede for a poor widow? M'sieur Pierre. Who will provide sober advice, who will recommend a medicine, who will bring glad tidings? Who? Who? M'sieur Pierre. All will be done by M'sieur Pierre."

"Remarkable! What talent!" exclaimed the director, as though he had been listening to poetry; yet all the time from beneath a twitching eyebrow he kept glancing at Cincinnatus.

"Therefore, it seems to me," went on M'sieur Pierre, "Oh yes, by the way," he interrupted himself, "are you satisfied with your quarters? You are not cold at night? Do they give you enough to eat?"

"He gets the same as I," answered Rodrig Ivanovich. "The board is excellent."

"All aboard," quipped M'sieur Pierre.

The director was getting ready to roar again, but just then the door opened and the gloomy, lanky librarian appeared with a stack of books under his arm. A woolen scarf was wound around his throat. Without saying hello to anyone he dumped the books on the cot, and for a moment stereometric apparitions of those same books, composed of dust, hung above them in the air, they hung, vibrated, and dispersed.

"Wait a minute," said Rodrig Ivanovich. "I don't think you have met."

The librarian nodded, without looking, while polite M'sieur Pierre rose from his chair.

"Please, M'sieur Pierre," begged the director, putting his hand to his shirt front, "please show him your trick!"

"Oh, it's hardly worth it—it's really nothing," M'sieur Pierre modestly began but the director would not stop:

"It's a miracle! Red magic! We all beg you! Oh, do it for us . . . Wait, wait just a minute," he shouted to the librarian, who was already starting toward the door. "Just a minute, M'sieur Pierre will show you something. Please, please! Don't go . . ."

"Think of one of these cards," pronounced M'sieur Pierre with mock solemnity; he shuffled the deck; he threw out the five of spades.

"No," said the librarian and left.

M'sieur Pierre shrugged a round little shoulder.

"I'll be right back," muttered the director and went out also.

Cincinnatus and his guest remained alone.

Cincinnatus opened a book and buried himself in it, that is, he kept reading the first sentence over and over. M'sieur Pierre looked at him with a kind smile, with one little paw lying palm up on the table, just as if he were offering to make peace with Cincinnatus. The director returned. In his tightly clenched fist was a woolen scarf.

"Maybe you can use it, M'sieur Pierre," he said; then he handed over the scarf, sat down, exhaled noisily like a horse, and began examining his thumb, from the end of which a half-broken nail protruded like a sickle.

"What were we talking about?" exclaimed M'sieur Pierre with charming tact, just as if nothing had happened. "Yes, we were talking about photographs. Some time I'll bring my camera and take your picture. That will be fun. What are you reading? May I take a look?"

"You ought to put the book aside," remarked the director with a rasp of exasperation in his voice; "after all, you do have a guest."

"Oh, let him be," smiled M'sieur Pierre.

There was a pause.

"It is growing late," said the director after consulting his watch.

"Yes, we'll be going in a minute ... My, what a little grouch ... Look at him, his little lips all atremble ... any moment now the sun will peek out from behind the clouds ... Grouch, grouch! ..."

"Let's go," said the director, rising.

"Just a moment ... I like it so much here that I can

hardly tear myself away . . . In any case, my dear neighbor, I shall take advantage of your permission to visit you often, often—that is, of course, if you grant me permission—and you will, won't you? . . . Good-by for now, then. Good-by! Good-by!"

Bowing comically, in imitation of someone, M'sieur Pierre withdrew; the director once again took him by his elbow, emitting voluptuous nasal sounds. They left, but at the last minute his voice was heard to say: "Excuse me, I forgot something, I'll catch up with you in a moment," and the director gushed back into the cell; he approached Cincinnatus, and for an instant the smile left his purple face: "I am ashamed," he hissed through his teeth, "ashamed of you. You behaved like . . . I'm coming, I'm coming," he yelled, beaming once again; then he snatched the vase of peonies from the table, and splashing water as he went, left the cell.

Cincinnatus kept staring into the book. A drop had fallen on the page. Through the drop several letters turned from brevier into pica, having swollen as if a reading glass were lying over them.

Eight

(There are some who sharpen a pencil toward themselves, as if they were peeling a potato, and there are others who slice away from themselves, as though whittling a stick ... Rodion was of the latter number. He had an old penknife with several blades and a corkscrew. The corkscrew slept on the outside.)

"Today is the eighth day" (wrote Cincinnatus with the pencil, which had lost more than a third of its length) "and not only am I still alive, that is, the sphere of my own self still limits and eclipses my being, but, like any other mortal, I do not know my mortal hour and can apply to myself a formula that holds for everyone: the probability of a future decreases in inverse proportion to its theoretical remoteness. Of course in my case discretion requires that I think in term of very small numbers—but that is all right, that is all right—I am alive. I had a strange sensation last night—and it was not the first time—: I am taking off layer after layer, until at last . . . I do not know how to describe it, but I know this: through the process of gradual divestment I reach the final, indivisible, firm, radiant point, and this point says: I am! like a pearl ring embedded in a shark's gory fat—O my eternal, my eternal . . . and this point is enough for me—actually nothing more is necessary. Perhaps as a citizen of the next century, a guest who has arrived ahead of time (the hostess is not yet up), perhaps simply a carnival freak in a gaping, hopelessly festive world, I have lived an agonizing life, and I would like to describe that agony to you—but I am obsessed by the fear that there will not be time enough. As far back as I can remember myself—and I remember myself with lawless lucidity, I have been my own accomplice, who knows too much, and therefore is dangerous. I issue from such burning blackness, I spin like a top, with such propelling force, such tongues of flame, that to this day I occasionally feel (sometimes during sleep, sometimes while immersing myself in very hot water) that primordial palpitation of mine, that first branding contact, the mainspring of my "I." How I wriggled out, slippery, naked! Yes, from a realm forbidden and inaccessible to others, yes. I know something, yes . . . but even now, when it is all over anyway, even now—I am afraid that I may corrupt someone? Or will nothing come of what I am trying to tell, its only vestiges being the corpses of strangled words, like hanged men . . . evening silhouettes of gammas and gerunds, gallow crows—

I think I should prefer the rope, since I know authoritatively and irrevocably that it shall be the ax; a little time gained, time, which is now so precious to me that I value every respite, every postponement . . . I mean time allotted to thinking; the furlough I allow my thoughts for a free journey from fact to fantasy and return . . . I mean much more besides, but lack of writing skill, haste, excitement, weakness . . . I know something. I know something. But expression of it comes so hard! No, I cannot . . . I would like to give up—yet I have the feeling of boiling and rising, a tickling, which may drive you mad if you do not express it somehow. Oh no, I do not gloat over my own person, I do not get all hot wrestling with my soul in a darkened room; I have no desires, save the desire to express myself— in defiance of all the world's muteness. How frightened I am. How sick with fright. But no one shall take me away from myself. I am frightened—and now I am losing some thread, which I held so palpably only a moment ago. Where is it? It has slipped out of my grasp! I am trembling over the paper, chewing the pencil through to the lead, hunching over to conceal myself from the door through which a piercing eye stings me in the nape, and it seems I am right on the verge of crumpling everything and tearing it up. I am here through an error—not in this prison, specifically—but in this whole terrible, striped world; a world which seems not a bad example of amateur craftsmanship, but is in reality calamity, horror, madness, error— and look, the curio slays the tourist, the gigantic carved bear brings its wooden mallet down upon me. And yet, ever since early childhood, I have had dreams . . . In my dreams the world was ennobled, spiritualized; people whom in the waking state I feared so much appeared there in a shimmering refraction, just as if they were imbued with and enveloped by that vibration of light which in sultry weather inspires the very outlines of objects with life; their voices, their step, the expressions of their eyes and even of their clothes—acquired an exciting significance; to put it more simply, in my dreams the world would come alive, becoming so captivatingly majestic, free and ethereal, that afterwards it would be oppressive to breathe the dust of this painted life. But then I have long since grown accustomed to the thought that what we call dreams is semi-reality, the promise of reality, a foreglimpse and a whiff of it; that is, they contain, in a very vague, diluted state, more genuine reality than our vaunted waking life which, in its turn, is semi-sleep, an evil drowsiness into which penetrate in grotesque disguise the sounds and sights of the real world, flowing beyond the periphery of the mind—as when you hear during sleep a dreadful insidious tale because a branch is scraping on the pane, or see yourself sinking into snow because your blanket is sliding off. But how I fear awakening! How I fear that second, or rather split second, already cut short then, when, with a lumberjack's grunt—But what is there to fear? Will it not be for me simply the shadow of an ax, and shall I not hear the downward vigorous grunt with the ear of a different world? Still I am afraid! One cannot write it off so easily. Neither is it good that my thoughts keep getting sucked into the cavity of the future— I want to think about something else, clarify other things . . . but I write obscurely and limply, like Pushkin's lyrical duelist. Soon, I think, I shall evolve a third eye on the back of my neck, between my brittle vertebrae: a mad eye, wide open, with a dilating pupil and pink venation on the glossy ball. Keep away! Even stronger, more hoarsely: hands off! I can foresee it all! And how often do my ears ring with the sob I am destined to emit and the terrible gurgling cough, uttered by the beheaded tyro. But all of this is not the point, and my discourse on dreams and waking are also not the point . . . Wait! There, I feel once again that I shall really express myself, shall bring the words to bay. Alas, no one taught me this kind of chase, and the ancient inborn art of writing is long since forgotten—forgotten are the days when it needed no schooling, but ignited and blazed like a forest fire—today it seems just as incredible as the music that once used to be extracted from a monstrous pianoforte, music that would nimbly ripple or suddenly hack the world into great, gleaming blocks—I myself picture all this so clearly, but you are not I, and therein lies the irreparable calamity. Not knowing how to write, but sensing with my criminal intuition how words are combined, what one must do for a commonplace word to come alive and to share its neighbor's sheen, heat, shadow, while reflecting itself in its neighbor and renewing the neighboring word in the process, so that the whole line is live iridescence; while I sense the nature of this kind of word propinquity, I am nevertheless unable to achieve it, yet that is what is indispensable to me for my task, a task of not now and not here. Not here! The horrible 'here,' the dark dungeon, in which a relentlessly howling heart is encarcerated, this 'here' holds and constricts me. But what gleams shine through at night, and what—. It exists, my dream world, it must exist, since, surely there must be an original of the clumsy copy. Dreamy, round, and blue, it turns slowly toward me. It is as if you are lying supine, with eyes closed, on an overcast day, and suddenly the gloom stirs under your eyelids, and slowly becomes first a langorous smile, then a warm feeling of contentment, and you know that the sun has come out from behind the clouds. With just such a feeling my world begins: the misty air gradually clears, and it is suffused with such radiant, tremulous kindness, and my soul expanses so freely in its native realm.—But then what, then what? Yes, that is the line beyond which I lose control . . . Brought up into the air, the word bursts, as burst those spherical fishes that breathe and blaze only in the compressed murk of the depths when brought up in the net. However I am making one last effort—and I think I have caught my prey . . . but it is only a fleeting apparition of my prey! *There, tam, là-bas,* the gaze of men glows with inimitable understanding; *there* the freaks that are tortured here walk unmolested; *there* time takes shape according to one's pleasure, like a figured rug whose folds can be gathered in such a way that two designs will meet—and the rug is once again smoothed out, and you live on, or else superimpose the next image on the last, endlessly, endlessly, with the leisurely concentration of a woman selecting a belt to go with her dress—now she glides in my direction, rhythmically butting the velvet with her knees, comprehending everything and comprehensible to me . . . *There, there* are the originals of those gardens where we used to roam and hide in this world; *there* everything strikes one by its bewitching evidence, by the simplicity of perfect good; *there* everything pleases one's soul, everything is filled with the kind of fun that children know; *there* shines the mirror that now and then sends a chance reflection here . . . And what I say is not it, not quite it, and I am getting mixed up, getting nowhere, talking nonsense, and the more I move about and search in the water where I grope on the sandy bottom for a glimmer I have glimpsed, the muddier the water grows, and the less likely it becomes that I shall grasp it. No, I have as yet said nothing, or, rather, said only bookish words . . . and in the end the logical thing would be to give up and I would give up if I were laboring for a reader existing today, but as there is in the world not a single human who can speak my language; or, more simply, not a single human who can speak; or, even more simply, not a single human; I must think only of myself, of that force which urges me to express myself. I am cold, weakened, afraid, the back of my head blinks and cringes, and once again gazes with insane intensity, but, in spite of everything, I am chained to this table like a cup to a drinking fountain, and will not rise till I have said what I want. I repeat (gathering new momentum in the rhythm of repetitive incantations), I repeat: there is something I know, there is something I know, there is something . . . When still a child, living still in a canary-yellow, large, cold house where they were preparing me and hundreds of other children for secure nonexistence as adult dummies, into which all my coevals turned without effort or pain; already then, in those accursed days, amid rag books and brightly painted school materials and soul-chilling drafts, I knew without knowing, I knew without wonder, I knew as one knows oneself, I knew what it is impossible to know—and, I would say, I knew it even more clearly than I do now. For life has worn me down: continual uneasiness, concealment of my knowledge, pretense, fear, a painful straining of all my nerves—not to let down, not to ring out ... and even to this day I still feel an ache in that part of my memory where the very beginning of this effort is recorded, that is, the occasion when I first understood that things which to me had seemed natural were actually forbidden, impossible, that any thought of them was criminal. Well do I remember that day! I must have just learned how to make letters, since I remember myself wearing on my fifth finger the little copper ring that was given to children who already knew how to copy the model words from the flower beds in the school garden, where petunias, phlox and marigold spelled out lengthy adages. I was sitting with my feet up on the low window sill and looking down as my schoolmates, dressed in the same kind of long pink smocks as I, held hands and circled around a beribboned pole. Why was I left out? In punishment? No. Rather, the reluctance of the other children to have me in their game and the mortal embarrassment, shame and dejection I myself felt when I joined them made me prefer that white nook of the sill, sharply marked off by the shadow of the half-open casement. I could hear the exclamations required by the game and the strident commands of the red-haired 'pedagoguette'; I could see her curls and her spectacles, and with the squeamish horror that never left me I watched her give the smallest children shoves to make them whirl faster. And that teacher, and the striped pole, and the white clouds, now and then letting through the gliding sun, which would suddenly spill out passionate light, searching for something, were all repeated in the flaming glass of the open window ... In short, I felt such fear and sadness that I tried to submerge within myself, to slow down and slip out of the senseless life that was carrying me onward. Just then, at the end of the stone gallery where I was sitting, appeared the senior educator—I do not recall his name—a fat, sweaty, shaggy-chested man, who was on his way to the bathing place. While still at a distance he shouted to me, his voice amplified by the acoustics, to go into the garden; he approached quickly and flourished his towel. In my sadness, in my abstraction, unconsciously and innocently, instead of descending into the garden by the stairs (the gallery was on the third floor), not thinking what I was doing, but really acting obediently, even submissively, I stepped straight from the window sill onto the elastic air and—feeling nothing more than a half-sensation of bare-footedness (even though I had shoes on)—slowly and quite naturally strode forward, still absently sucking and examining the finger in which I had caught a splinter that morning ... Suddenly, however, an extraordinary, deafening silence brought me out of my reverie, and I saw below me, like pale daisies, the upturned faces of the stupefied children, and the pedagoguette, who seemed to be falling backward; I saw also the globes of the trimmed shrubs, and the falling towel that had not yet reached the lawn; I saw myself, a pink-smocked boy, standing transfixed in mid-air; turning around, I saw, but three aerial paces from me, the window I had just left, and, his hairy arm extended in malevolent amazement, the—"

(Here, unfortunately, the light in the cell went out—Rodion always turned it off exactly at ten.)

Nine

And again the day began with a din of voices. Rodion was gloomily giving instructions, and three other attendants were assisting him. The entire family of Marthe had arrived for the interview, bringing with them all their furniture. Not thus, not thus had he imagined this long-awaited meeting ... How they lumbered in! Marthe's aged father, with his huge bald head, and bags under his eyes, and the rubbery tap of his black cane; Marthe's brothers, identical twins except that one had a golden mustache and the other a pitch-black one; Marthe's maternal grandparents, so old that one could already see through them; three vivacious female cousins, who, however, were not admitted for some reason at the last minute; Marthe's children—lame Diomedon and obese little Pauline; at last Marthe herself, wearing her best black dress, with a velvet ribbon around her cold white neck, and holding a hand mirror; a very proper young man with a flawless profile was constantly at her side.

The father-in-law, leaning on his stick, seated himself in a leather armchair that had arrived with him, with an effort put a fat suede foot up on a stool and, angrily shaking his head, fixed his gaze, from beneath heavy eyelids, on Cincinnatus, who felt the familiar dull sensation at the sight of the frogs ornamenting the father-in-law's warm jacket, the folds around his mouth that seemed to express eternal disgust, and the purple blotch of a birthmark on his corded temple, with a swelling resembling a big raisin right on the vein.

The grandfather and grandmother (the one all shaky and shriveled, in patched trousers, the other with her white hair bobbed, and so slim that she might have encased herself in a silk umbrella sheath) settled side by side in two identical high-backed chairs; the grandfather tightly clutched in his small hirsute hands a bulky portrait, in a gilt frame, of his mother, a misty young woman, in turn holding a portrait.

Meanwhile, furniture, household utensils, even individual sections of walls continued to arrive. There came a mirrored wardrobe, bringing with it its own private reflection (namely, a corner of the connubial bedroom with a stripe of sunlight across the floor, a dropped glove, and an open door in the distance.) A cheerless little tricycle with orthopedic attachments was rolled in. It was followed by the inlaid table which had supported a flat garnet flacon and a hairpin for the last ten years. Marthe sat down on her black couch, embroidered with roses.

"Woe, woe!" proclaimed the father-in-law, striking the floor with his cane. Frightened little smiles appeared on the faces of the oldsters. "Don't, daddy, we've been through it a thousand times," Marthe said quietly, and shrugged a chilly shoulder. Her young man offered her a fringed shawl but she, forming the rudiment of a tender smile with one corner of her thin lips, waved away his sensitive hand. ("The first thing I look at in a man is his hands.") He was dressed in the smart black uniform of a telegraph employee and perfumed with violet scent.

"Woe!" repeated the father-in-law forcefully and began to curse Cincinnatus in detail and with relish. Cincinnatus's gaze was drawn to Pauline's green polka-dotted dress: red-haired, cross-eyed, bespectacled, arousing not laughter but sadness with those polka dots and that plumpness, dully moving her fat legs in brown wool stockings and button shoes, she would approach those present and study each, gazing gravely and silently with her small dark eyes, which seemed to meet behind the bridge of her nose. The poor thing had a napkin tied around her neck—evidently they had forgotten to take it off after breakfast.

The father-in-law paused to regain breath, then struck another blow with his cane, whereupon Cincinnatus said, "Yes, I am listening."

"Silence, insolent fellow," shouted the former, "I am entitled to expect from you—if only today, when you stand at death's door—a little respect. How you managed to get

yourself on the block . . . I want an explanation from you
—how you could . . . how you dared . . ."

Marthe asked her young man something in a low voice;
he was carefully rummaging around, probing all around
himself and under himself on the couch; "no, no, it's all
right," he answered just as softly, "I must have dropped it
on the way . . . Don't worry, it'll turn up . . . But tell me,
are you sure you're not cold?" Shaking her head negatively,
Marthe lowered her soft palm onto his wrist; and, taking
her hand away immediately, she straightened her dress
across the knees and in a harsh whisper called her son, who
was bothering his uncles, who in turn kept pushing him
away—he was preventing them from listening. Diomedon,
in a gray blouse with an elastic at the hips, twisting his
whole body in a rhythmic distortion, nevertheless quite
rapidly covered the distance between them and his mother.
His left leg was healthy and rosy; the right one resembled a
rifle in its complicated harness: barrel, straps, sling. His
round hazel eyes and sparse eyebrows were his mother's,
but the lower half of his face, with its bulldog jowls—this,
of course, was someone else's. "Sit here," whispered Marthe
and, with a quick slap arrested the hand mirror which was
trickling off the couch.

"You tell me," the father-in-law was continuing, "how
you dared, you, a happy family man—splendid furniture,
wonderful children, a loving wife—how you dared not consider all this, you villain? It seems to me sometimes that
I am no more than an old moron and understand nothing,
because otherwise I must allow for such loathsomeness
. . . Silence!" he roared, and again the oldsters started and
smiled.

A black cat stretched, straining back one hind paw, rubbed itself against Cincinnatus's leg, then was suddenly on the sideboard, and from there noiselessly leaped onto the shoulder of the lawyer who, having just tiptoed in, was sitting in a corner on a plush hassock—he had a bad cold and, over a handkerchief held ready for use, was inspecting the assembled company and the various household items that made the cell look like the site of an auction; the cat startled him, and he threw it off with a convulsive movement.

The father-in-law was thundering on, multiplying curses and already beginning to grow hoarse. Marthe placed her hand over her eyes; her young man, tensing his jaw muscles, was watching her. On a settee with a curved back sat Marthe's brothers; the dark one, in a tawny suit and open shirt collar, was holding music paper rolled into a tube and as yet bearing no music—he was one of the city's foremost singers; his twin, in sky-blue plus-fours, a dandy and a wit, had brought a present for his brother-in-law—a bowl of bright fruit made of wax. He had also fixed a crepe arm band on his sleeve and kept indicating it with his finger as he tried to catch Cincinnatus's eye.

At the peak of his eloquence the father-in-law suddenly choked and gave his chair such a wrench that quiet little Pauline, who had been standing by him and looking at his mouth, toppled backwards behind the chair, where she lay still, hoping that nobody noticed. With a crackle the father-in-law began opening a cigarette box. Everyone was quiet.

The various trampled sounds began to straighten up.

Marthe's brother, the brunet, cleared his throat and softly began to sing "*Mali é trano t'amesti. . . .*" He stopped short and looked at his brother, who made terrible eyes at him. The lawyer, smiling at something, again applied himself to his handkerchief. On the couch, Marthe was talking in a whisper with her escort, who was pleading with her to throw the shawl over herself—the prison air was a little damp. When they spoke they used the formal second person plural, but with what a cargo of tenderness this second person plural was laden as it sailed along the horizon of their barely audible conversation . . . The little old man, trembling awfully, got up from his chair, handed the portrait to his old woman and, shielding the flame that was trembling like himself, went up to Cincinnatus's father-in-law, and was going to light his . . . But the flame went out, and the latter frowned angrily.

"You have really become a nuisance with your stupid lighter," said he glumly, but already without wrath; then the atmosphere really grew animated, and everybody began talking simultaneously. "*Mali é trano t'amesti!*" Marthe's brother sang full voice; "Diomedon, leave the cat alone this instant," said Marthe. "You already strangled one the other day, one every day is too much. Take it away from him, please, Victor, dear." Availing herself of the general animation, Pauline crawled out from behind the chair and quietly got up. The lawyer walked over to Cincinnatus's father-in-law and gave him a light.

"Take the word 'anxiety,' " Cincinnatus's brother-in-law, the wit, was saying to him. "Now take away the word 'tiny', Eh? Comes out funny, doesn't it? Yes, friend, you've really got yourself in a mess. In truth, what made you do such a thing?"

Meanwhile the door opened imperceptibly. M'sieur Pierre and the director stood on the threshold, hands clasped identically behind their backs, and quietly, delicately moving only their eyeballs, were examining the assemblage. They stood and looked like this for more than a minute before leaving.

"Listen to me," the brother-in-law was saying, breathing hotly. "I'm your old pal. Do as I say. Repent, my little Cincinnatus. Come on, do me this favor. You don't know, they might still let you off. Eh? Think how unpleasant it is to have your chump lopped off. What do you have to lose? Come on—don't be a blockhead."

"Greetings, greetings, greetings," said the lawyer, coming over to Cincinnatus. "Don't embrace me, I still have a bad cold. What is the conversation about? How can I be of service?"

"Let me pass," murmured Cincinnatus, "I have to say a couple of words to my wife . . ."

"Now, my dearest, let us discuss the question of property," said the father-in-law, refreshed, and extended his cane in such a way that Cincinnatus stumbled over it. "Wait, wait a minute, I am speaking to you!"

Cincinnatus kept going; he had to get around a large table, set for ten persons, and then squeeze between the screen and the wardrobe in order to reach Marthe, who reclined on the couch. The young man had covered her feet with the shawl. Cincinnatus almost made it, but just then there was an angry shriek from Diomedon. He turned

around and saw Emmie, who had entered in some unknown way and was now teasing the boy: imitating his
lameness, she was dragging one leg with various complicated contortions. Cincinnatus caught her by the arm, but
she broke loose and ran off. Pauline waddled after her in a
silent ecstasy of curiosity. Marthe turned to him. The young man very correctly
stood up. "Marthe, just a couple of words, I beg you," said
Cincinnatus rapidly; he tripped over the cushion on the
floor and sat down awkwardly on the edge of the couch, at
the same time wrapping his ash-smeared dressing gown
around himself. "A slight migraine," said the young man.
"What can you expect? Such excitement is bad for her."
"You are right," said Cincinnatus. "Yes, you are right. I
should like to ask you . . . I must—in private—" "Beg pardon, sir," said the voice of Rodion close to him. Cincinnatus stood up; Rodion and another employee, looking each
other in the eye, grasped the couch on which Marthe was
reclining, grunted, picked it up and carried it toward the
door. "Good-by, good-by," Marthe called childishly, swaying in time with the step of the porters, but suddenly she
closed her eyes and covered her face. Her escort walked
solicitously behind, carrying the black shawl he had picked
up from the floor, a bouquet, his uniform cap, and a solitary glove. There was commotion all around. The brothers
were packing the dishes in a trunk. Their father, breathing
asthmatically, was overcoming the multisegmented screen.
The lawyer was offering everyone a vast sheet of wrapping
paper obtained by him from some unknown source; he was
seen unsuccessfully attempting to wrap in it a bowl con-

taining a pale-orange little fish in clouded water. Amid the commotion the ample wardrobe with its private reflection stood like a pregnant woman, carefully holding and turning aside its glass belly so no one would brush against it. It was tilted backward and, in a reeling hug, carried away. People were coming up to Cincinnatus to say good-by. "Well, let's let bygones be bygones," said the father-in-law and, with cold politeness, kissed Cincinnatus's hand as custom demanded. The blond brother sat the dark one on his shoulders and in that position they took leave of Cincinnatus and departed, like a live mountain. The grandparents were shivering, bowing and holding up the hazy portrait. The employees kept carrying out the furniture. The children approached: Solemn Pauline raised up her face; Diomedon, on the contrary, gazed down at the floor. The lawyer led them away by their respective hands. The last to fly up to him was Emmie, pale, tear-stained, her nose pink and her mouth wet and quivering; she was silent, but suddenly, with a slight crackle, she rose on her toes, twined her hot arms around his neck, whispered incoherently and uttered a loud sob. Rodion seized her by the wrist—judging by his grumbling he had been calling her for a long time; now he dragged her firmly toward the exit. Arching back her body, turning toward Cincinnatus her head with its streaming hair and extending to him, palm upturned, her lovely arm (with the appearance of a ballet captive but with the shadow of genuine despair), Emmie unwillingly followed Rodion as he dragged her; her eyes kept rolling back, her shoulder strap slipped off, and now, with a swinging motion, as though he were emptying a water bucket, he splashed her out into the corridor. Then, still muttering, he returned with a dustpan to pick up the corpse of the cat that lay flat under a chair. The door slammed with a crash. It was now hard to believe that in this cell, only a moment ago—

Ten

"When the lone wolf cub gets better acquainted with my views he will stop shying away from me. A certain amount of progress, however, has already been achieved, and I welcome it with all my heart," M'sieur Pierre was saying, seated sidewise to the table as was his wont, his plump calves compactly crossed, and one hand playing soundless chords on the oilcloth. Cincinnatus, his head propped on his hand, lay on the cot.

"We are alone now, and it's raining," went on M'sieur Pierre; "Such weather is ideal for intimate chit-chat. Let us settle once for all . . . I get the impression that you are surprised, even irritated by the administration's attitude toward me; it is as if I were in a privileged position—no, no, don't argue—let us have it out. Allow me to tell you two things. You know our dear director (by the way, the wolf cub is not entirely fair to him, but we'll talk about that later), you know how impressionable he is, how enthusiastic, how he is carried away with every novelty—I think he must have been carried away with you the first few days— so the passion that now inflames him for me need not upset you. Let's not be so jealous, my friend. In the second place, strangely enough, you are evidently still unaware of why I ended up here, but when I tell you, there are many things you will understand. Excuse me, what is that you have on your neck—right here, here—yes, here."

"Where?" Cincinnatus asked mechanically, feeling his neck vertebrae.

M'sieur Pierre went over to him and sat down on the edge of the cot. "Right here," he said, "but I see now that it was only a shadow. I thought I saw . . . a little swelling of some kind. You seem uncomfortable when you move your head. Does it hurt? Did you catch a chill?"

"Oh, stop pestering me, please," Cincinnatus said, sorrowfully.

"No, just a minute. My hands are clean—allow me to feel here. It seems, after all . . . Does it hurt here? How about here?"

With his small but muscular hand he was rapidly touching Cincinnatus's neck and examining it carefully, breathing through the nose with a slight wheeze.

"No, nothing. Everything is in order," he said at last, moving away and slapping the patient on the nape—"Only you do have an awfully thin one—otherwise everything is normal, it's just that sometimes, you know . . . Let's see your tongue. The tongue is a mirror of the stomach. Cover up, cover up, it's chilly in here. What were we chatting about? Refresh my memory."

"If you were really interested in my welfare," said Cincinnatus, "then you would leave me alone. Go away, please."

"You mean you really do not want to hear what I have to say," M'sieur Pierre objected with a smile, "you really are so obstinately convinced that your conclusions are infallible—conclusions that are unknown to me—mark that, unknown."

Lost in sadness, Cincinnatus said nothing.

"Allow me to tell you, though," M'sieu Pierre went on with a certain solemnity, "what was the nature of my crime. I was accused—justly or not, that is a different matter—I was accused . . . of what, do you suppose?"

"Well, come on out with it," said Cincinnatus with a melancholy sigh.

"You will be amazed. I was accused of attempting to . . . Oh ungrateful, distrustful friend . . . I was accused of attempting to help you escape from here."

"Is that true?" asked Cincinnatus.

"I never lie," M'sieur Pierre said imposingly. "Perhaps there are times when one ought to lie—that is another matter—and perhaps such scrupulous veracity is foolish and in the end does no good—that may all be so. But the fact remains, I never lie. I ended up here, my fine friend, because of you. I was arrested at night. Where? Let us say in Upper Elderbury. Yes, I am an Elderburian. Salt works, fruit orchards. Should you ever want to come and call on me, I shall treat you to some of our elderburies (I assume no responsibility for the pun—it appears in our city seal). There—

not in the seal, but in the jail—your obedient servant spent three days. Then they transferred me here."

"You mean you wanted to save me . . ." Cincinnatus said pensively.

"Whether I wanted to or not is my business, friend of my heart, cockroach-under-the-hearth. In any case I was accused of it—you know, informers are a young and hotheaded breed, so here I am: 'here in rapture I'm standing before you . . .'—remember the song? The principal evidence against me was some sketch of this fortress that supposedly had my marks on it. You see, I was supposed to have thought out every last detail of your escape, my little cockroach."

"You were supposed to, or . . . ?" asked Cincinnatus.

"What a naïve, delightful creature he is!" grinned M'sieur Pierre, displaying a multitude of teeth. "He wants everything to be so simple—as, alas, it never is in real life!"

"One would still like to know," said Cincinnatus.

"What? Whether my judges were right? Whether I really was planning to save you? Shame, shame . . ."

"Then it is true?" whispered Cincinnatus.

M'sieur Pierre got up and began to walk about the cell. "Let us leave the matter," he said resignedly. "Decide for yourself, distrustful friend. One way or another, but I ended up here because of you. And I'll tell you more: we shall mount the scaffold together too."

He kept walking about the cell with a noiseless, springy step, the soft parts of his body, enclosed in prison pajamas, bouncing slightly, and Cincinnatus, with dejected attention, followed every step of the nimble fatty.

"For the heck of it I shall believe you," Cincinnatus said

finally, "We'll see what will come of it. You hear me, I believe you. And, to make it more convincing, I even thank you."

"Oh, what for—there's no need . . ." said M'sieur Pierre and sat down again by the table. "I simply wanted you to be informed. That's fine. Now we've both got a load off our chests, haven't we? I don't know about you, but I feel like crying. And this is a good feeling. Cry, do not restrain those salutary tears."

"How horrible it is here," said Cincinnatus cautiously.

"There's nothing horrible about it. By the way, I've wanted to reproach you for a long time about your attitude toward the life here. No, no, don't turn away, allow me, as a friend . . . You are not fair either to our good Rodion or, even more important, to his excellency the director. All right—he is not very bright, a little pompous, something of a scatterbrain—and he is not adverse to delivering speeches—it's all true, and I myself sometimes am not in the mood for him and, of course, cannot share with him my inmost thoughts, as I do with you, especially when my soul—pardon the expression—aches. But whatever faults he might have, he is a straight-forward, honest and kind man. Yes, a man of rare kindness—do not argue—I would not say it if I did not know, and I never speak idly, and I have more experience and know life and people better than you. That's why it hurts me to see with what cruel coldness, what haughty contempt you reject Rodrig Ivanovich. I can sometimes read such pain in his eyes . . . As for Rodion, how is that you who are so intelligent are unable to perceive through his assumed gruffness all the touching benignity of this grown-up child. Oh, I realize that you are nervous, that you are sex starved—still, Cincinnatus—you'll forgive me, but it isn't right, it isn't right at all ... And, in general, you slight people ... You scarcely touch the marvelous dinners we get here. All right, supposing you don't care for them—believe me, I too know a little about gastronomy—but you sneer at them, and yet someone cooked them, someone worked hard ... I know, it sometimes gets boring here, and you feel like going for a walk or having a romp—but why think only of yourself, of your desires, why haven't you smiled even once at the painstaking little jokes of dear pathetic Rodrig Ivanovich? ... Perhaps he cries afterwards, and does not sleep nights, remembering how you reacted ..."

"In any case your defense is clever," said Cincinnatus, "but I am an expert in dolls. I shall not yield."

"It's a pity," said M'sieur Pierre in a hurt tone. "I ascribe it to your youth," he added after a pause. "No, no, you must not be so unfair ..."

"Tell me," asked Cincinnatus, "do they keep you in the dark too? The fateful churl has not arrived yet? The hacking fest isn't set for tomorrow?"

"You should not use such words," remarked M'sieur Pierre confidentially. "Particularly with that intonation ... There is something vulgar in it, something unworthy of a gentleman. How can you pronounce such things—I am surprised at you ..."

"But tell me, when?" asked Cincinnatus.

"In due time," M'sieur Pierre replied evasively. "Why such foolish curiosity? And in general ... No, you still have a lot to learn—this sort of thing won't do. This arrogance, these preconceptions ..."

"But how they drag it out . . ." Cincinnatus said drowsily. "Of course one does get accustomed to it . . . You hold your soul in readiness from one day to the next—and still they will take you by surprise. Ten days have passed like this, and I haven't gone crazy. And then, of course, there is always some hope . . . Indistinct, as if under water, but therefore all the more attractive. You speak of escape . . . I think, I surmise, that there is someone else too who is concerned with it . . . Certain hints . . . But what if this is only deception, a fold of the fabric mimicking a human face . . ."

He sighed and paused.

"This is curious," said M'sieur Pierre. "What are these hopes, and who is this savior?"

"Imagination," replied Cincinnatus. "And you—would you like to escape?"

"What do you mean 'escape'? Where to?" asked M'sieur Pierre in amazement.

Cincinnatus sighed again.

"What difference does it make where? We might, you and I . . . I don't know, though, whether, with your build, you are able to run fast. Your legs . . ."

"Come, come, what kind of nonsense is that?" said M'sieur Pierre, squirming in his chair. "Only in fairy tales do people escape from prison. As for your remarks about my physique, kindly keep them to yourself."

"I feel sleepy," said Cincinnatus.

M'sieur Pierre rolled up his right sleeve. There appeared a tattoo. Under the wonderfully white skin his muscle bulged and rolled. He assumed a firm stance, grasped the chair with one hand, turned it upside down and slowly began lifting it. Swaying from the effort, he held it for a moment high above his head and slowly lowered it. This was only a preliminary.

Concealing his labored respiration, he wiped his hands long and carefully with a red handkerchief, while the spider, as the youngest member of the circus family, performed a simple trick above his web.

Throwing him the handkerchief, M'sieur Pierre shouted a French exclamation and suddenly was standing on his hands. His spherical head gradually became suffused with beautiful rosy blood; his left trouser leg slid down, exposing his ankle; his upside-down eyes—as happens with anyone in this position—looked like the eyes of an octopus.

"How about that?" he asked, bouncing back onto his feet and readjusting his clothes. From the corridor came a tumult of applause, and then, separately, the clown began to clap, loose-jointedly, as he walked—before beaning himself on the barrier.

"Well?" repeated M'sieur Pierre. "How's that for strength? And will my agility do? Or haven't you seen enough yet?"

In one leap M'sieur Pierre hopped up on the table, stood on his hands, and grasped the back of the chair in his teeth. The music paused breathlessly. M'sieur Pierre was lifting the chair, clenched firmly between his teeth; his tensed muscles were quivering; his jaw was creaking.

The door softly swung open, and there entered—in jack boots, with a whip, powdered and spotlit with blinding violet light—the circus director. "Sensational! A unique performance!" he whispered, and, taking off his top hat, he sat down by Cincinnatus.

Something gave, and M'sieur Pierre, releasing the chair

from his mouth, turned a somersault and was again standing on the floor. Apparently, however, not everything was well. He at once covered his mouth with his handkerchief, glanced quickly under the table, then inspected the chair, and suddenly seeing what he sought, attempted, with a subdued oath, to yank off the back of the chair his hinged denture, which was embedded there. Magnificently displaying all its teeth, it held on with a bulldog grip. Whereupon, without losing his head, M'sieur Pierre embraced the chair and departed with it.

Rodrig Ivanovich, who had noticed nothing, was applauding wildly. The arena, however, remained empty. He cast a suspicious look at Cincinnatus, clapped some more, but without the former ardor, gave a little start and, in obvious distress, left the box.

And thus the performance ended.

Eleven

Now newspapers were no longer brought to
the cell: having noticed that everything that might have
any connection with the execution was clipped out, Cincinnatus himself had declined to receive them. Breakfast
had grown simpler: instead of chocolate—albeit weak chocolate—he would receive some slop with a flotilla of tea leaves;
the toast was so hard he could not bite through it. Rodion
made no secret of the fact that he had grown bored with
serving the silent and fastidious prisoner.

He would deliberately busy himself for a longer and
longer time in the cell. His flame-red beard, the imbecile
azure of his eyes, his leather apron, his clawlike hands—
all this accumulated through repetition to form such a de-

pressing, tedious impression that Cincinnatus would turn away toward the wall while the cleaning was in progress.

And that is how it was this day—only the return of the chair, with the deep imprints of bulldog teeth on the top edge of its straight back, served as a distinguishing feature for the day's beginning. Together with the chair Rodion brought a note from M'sieur Pierre; a fleecily curling script, elegant punctuation marks, signature like a seven-veil dance. In jocular and kindly words his neighbor thanked him for yesterday's friendly chat and expressed hope that it would be repeated shortly. "Let me assure you," thus ended the note, "that I am physically very, very strong [twice underlined with a ruler], and if you are still not convinced of this, I shall be honored some time to show you certain further interesting [underlined] demonstrations of agility and astounding muscular development."

After this, for two hours, with imperceptible intervals of mournful torpor, Cincinnatus, now pinching at his mustache, now flipping the pages of a book, walked about the cell. He had by now made a completely precise study of it— he knew it much better than, for instance, the room where he had lived for many years.

This is how matters stood with the walls: their number was unalterably four; they were painted a uniform yellow; but, because of the shadow covering it, the basic hue seemed dark and smooth, claylike as it were, in comparison with that shifting spot where the bright ochre reflection of the window spent the day: here, in the light, all the small protuberances of the thick yellow paint were in evidence— even the wavy curve of the tracings left by the joint passage of brush hairs—and there was the familiar scratch which the precious parallelogram of sunlight would reach at ten in the morning.

A creeping, heel-clutching chill rose from the dusky stone floor; an underdeveloped, mean little echo inhabited some part of the slightly concave ceiling, with a light (wire-enclosed) in its center—no, that is, not quite in the center: a flaw that agonizingly irritated the eye—and, in this sense, no less agonizing was the unsuccessful attempt to paint over the iron door.

Of the three items of furniture—cot, table, chair—only the last was movable. The spider also moved. Up above, where the sloping window recess began, the well-nourished black beastie had found points of support for a first-rate web with the same resourcefulness as Marthe displayed when she would find, in what seemed the most unsuitable corner, a place and a method for hanging out laundry to dry. Its paws folded so that the furry elbows stuck out at the sides, it would gaze with round hazel eyes at the hand with the pencil extended toward it, and would begin to back away, without taking its eyes off it. It was most eager however, to take a fly, or a moth from the large fingers of Rodion—and now, for example, in the southwest part of the web there hung a butterfly's orphaned hind wing, cherry-red, with a silky shading, and with blue lozenges along its crenelated edge. It stirred slightly in a delicate draft.

The inscriptions on the walls had by now been wiped away. The list of rules likewise had disappeared. Also taken away—or perhaps broken—was the classic pitcher with spelaean water in its resonant depths. All was bare, redoubtable, and cold in this chamber where the prisonlike character was suppressed by the neutrality of a waiting room—

whether office, hospital or some other kind—when it is already getting to be evening, and one hears only the humming in one's ears...and the horror of this waiting was somehow connected with the incorrectly located center of the ceiling.

Library volumes, in black shoe-leatherlike bindings, lay on the table, which had been covered for some time already with a checkered oilcloth. The pencil, which had lost its slender length and was well chewed, rested on violently scribbled pages, stacked windmill fashion. Here also had been thrown a letter to Marthe, completed by Cincinnatus the day before, that is, the day after the interview: but he could not make up his mind to send it, and had therefore let it lie a while, as though expecting from the thing itself that fruition which his irresolute thoughts, in need of another climate, simply could not achieve.

The subject will now be the precious quality of Cincinnatus; his fleshy incompleteness; the fact that the greater part of him was in a quite different place, while only an insignificant portion of it was wandering, perplexed, here—a poor, vague Cincinnatus, a comparatively stupid Cincinnatus, trusting, feeble and foolish as people are in their sleep. But even during this sleep—still, still—his real life showed through too much.

Cincinnatus's face, grown transparently pallid, with fuzz on its sunken cheeks and a mustache with such a delicate hair texture that it seemed to be actually a bit of disheveled sunlight on his upper lip; Cincinnatus's face, small and still young despite all the torments, with gliding eyes, eerie eyes of changeable shade, was, in regard to its expression, something absolutely inadmissible by the standards of his surroundings, especially now, when he had ceased to dissemble. The open shirt, the black dressing grown that kept flying open, the oversize slippers on his slender feet, the philosopher's skullcap on the top of his head and the ripple (there was a draft coming from somewhere after all!) running through the transparent hair on his temples completed a picture, the full indecency of which it is difficult to put into words—produced as it was of a thousand barely noticeable, overlapping trifles: of the light outline of his lips, seemingly not quite fully drawn but touched by a master of masters; of the fluttering movements of his empty, not-yet-shaded-in hands; of the dispersing and again gathering rays in his animated eyes; but even all of this, analyzed and studied, still could not fully explain Cincinnatus: it was as if one side of his being slid into another dimension, as all the complexity of a tree's foliage passes from shade into radiance, so that you cannot distinguish just where begins the submergence into the shimmer of a different element. It seemed as though at any moment, in the course of his movements about the limited space of the haphazardly invented cell, Cincinnatus would step in such a way as to slip naturally and effortlessly through some chink of the air into its unknown coulisses to disappear there with the same easy smoothness with which the flashing reflection of a rotated mirror moves across every object in the room and suddenly vanishes, as if beyond the air, in some new depth of ether. At the same time, everything about him breathed with a delicate, drowsy, but in reality exceptionally strong, ardent and independent life: his veins of the bluest blue pulsated; crystal-clear saliva moistened his lips; the skin quivered on his cheeks and his forehead, which was edged with dissolved light . . . and all this so teased the observer as to make him long to tear apart, cut to shreds, destroy utterly this brazen elusive flesh, and all that it implied and expressed, all that impossible, dazzling freedom—enough, enough—do not walk any more, Cincinnatus, lie down on your cot, so you will not arouse, will not irritate . . . And in truth Cincinnatus would become aware of the predatory eye in the peephole following him and lie down or sit at the table and open a book.

The black pile of books on the table consisted of the following: first, a contemporary novel that Cincinnatus had not bothered to read during his period of existence at liberty; second, one of those anthologies, published in countless editions with condensed rehashes of and excerpts from ancient literature; third, bound issues of an old magazine; fourth, several bedraggled little volumes of a work in an unknown tongue, brought him by mistake—he had not ordered them.

The novel was the famous *Quercus*, and Cincinnatus had already read a good third of it, or about a thousand pages. Its protagonist was an oak. The novel was a biography of that oak. At the place where Cincinnatus had stopped the oak was just starting on its third century; a simple calculation suggested that by the end of the book it would reach the age of six hundred at least.

The idea of the novel was considered to be the acme of modern thought. Employing the gradual development of the tree (growing lone and mighty at the edge of a canyon at whose bottom the waters never ceased to din), the author unfolded all the historic events—or shadows of events—of which the oak could have been a witness; now it was a dialogue between two warriors dismounted from their steeds —one dappled, the other dun—so as to rest under the cool ceil of its noble foliage; now highwaymen stopping by and the song of a wild-haired fugitive damsel; now, beneath the storm's blue zigzag, the hasty passage of a lord escaping from royal wrath; now, upon a spread cloak a corpse, still quivering with the throb of the leafy shadows; now a brief drama in the life of some villagers. There was a paragraph a page and a half long in which all the words began with "p."

It seemed as though the author were sitting with his camera somewhere among the topmost branches of the Quercus, spying out and catching his prey. Various images of life would come and go, pausing among the green macules of light. The normal periods of inaction were filled with scientific descriptions of the oak itself, from the viewpoints of dendrology, ornithology, coleopterology, mythology—or popular descriptions, with touches of folk humor. Among other things there was a detailed list of all the initials carved in the bark with their interpretations. And, finally, no little attention was devoted to the music of waters, the palette of sunsets, and the behavior of the weather.

Cincinnatus read for a while and laid it aside. This work was unquestionably the best that his age had produced; yet he overcame the pages with a melancholy feeling, plodded through the pages with dull distress, and kept drowning out the tale in the stream of his own meditation: what matters to me all this, distant, deceitful and dead—I, who am preparing to die? Or else he would begin imagining how the author, still a young man, living, so they said, on an island in the North Sea—would be dying himself; and it was somehow funny that eventually the author must needs die—and it was funny because the only real, genuinely unquestionable thing here was only death itself, the inevitability of the author's physical death. The light would move along the wall. Rodion would appear with what he called frühstück. Again a butterfly wing would slide between his fingers, leaving colored powder on them.

"Can it be that *he* has not arrived yet?" asked Cincinnatus; it was already not the first time he had asked this question, which greatly angered Rodion, and again he did not reply.

"And another interview—will they grant me that?" asked Cincinnatus.

In anticipation of the usual heartburn he lay down on the cot and, turning toward the wall, for a long, long time helped patterns form on it, from tiny blobs of the glossy paint and their round little shadows; he would discover, for example, a diminutive profile with a large mouselike ear; then he would lose it and was unable to reconstruct it. This cold ochre smelled of the grave, it was pimply and horrible, yet his gaze still persisted in selecting and correlating the necessary little protuberances—so starved he was for even a vague semblance of a human face. Finally he turned over, lay on his back and, with the same attention began to examine the shadows and cracks on the ceiling.

"Anyway, they have succeeded in softening me," mused Cincinnatus. "I have grown so limp and soggy that they will be able to do it with a fruit knife."

For some time he sat on the edge of the cot, his hands

compressed between his knees, all hunched over. Letting out a shuddering sigh he began again to roam. It is interesting, though, in what language this is written. The small, crowded, ornate type, with dots and squiggles within the sickle-shaped letters, seemed to be oriental—it was somehow reminiscent of the inscriptions on museum daggers. Such old little volumes, with their faded pages ... some tinged with tawny blotches.

The clock struck seven, and shortly Rodion appeared with dinner.

"You are sure *he* still has not come?" asked Cincinnatus.

Rodion was about to leave, but turned on the threshold.

"Shame on you," he said with a sob in his voice, "day and night you do nothing ... a body feeds you here, tends you lovingly, wears himself out for your sake, and all you do is ask stupid questions. For shame, you thankless man ..."

Time, humming evenly, continued to pass. The air in the cell grew dark, and when it had become quite dense and dull, the light came on in business-like fashion in the center of the ceiling—no, not quite in the center, that was just it—an agonizing reminder. Cincinnatus undressed and got in bed with *Quercus*. The author was already getting to the civilized ages, to judge by the conversation of three merry wayfarers, Tit, Pud, and the Wandering Jew who were taking swigs of wine from their flasks on the cool moss beneath the black vespertine oak.

"Will no one save me?" Cincinnatus suddenly asked aloud and sat up on the bed (opening his pauper's hands, showing that he had nothing).

"Can it be that no one will?" repeated Cincinnatus,

gazing at the implacable yellowness of the walls and still holding up his empty palms.

The draft became a leafy breeze. From the dense shadows above there fell and bounced on the blanket a large dummy acorn, twice as large as life, splendidly painted a glossy buff, and fitting its cork cup as snugly as an egg.

Twelve

He was awakened by a muted tapping, scratching, and the sound of something crumbling somewhere. Just as when, having fallen asleep healthy last night, you wake up past midnight in a fever. He listened to these sounds for quite a long while—trup, trup, tock-tock-tock—without any thought about their meaning, simply listening, because they had awakened him and because his hearing had nothing else to do. Trup, tap, scratch, crumble-crumble. Where? To the right? To the left? Cincinnatus raised himself up a little.

He listened—his whole head became an organ of hearing, his whole body a tense heart; he listened and already began to make sense out of certain indications: the weak distilla-

127 ₰

tion of darkness within the cell ... the dark had settled to the bottom ... Beyond the bars of the window, a gray twilight—that meant it was three or half past three ... The guards asleep in the cold ... The sounds were coming from somewhere below ... no, it was, rather, from above, no, it was still below, just on the other side of the wall, at floor level, like a large mouse scratching with iron claws.

Cincinnatus was especially excited by the concentrated self-confidence of the sounds, the insistent seriousness with which they pursued, in the quiet of the fortress night, perhaps a distant, but none the less attainable goal. With bated breath, with a phantomlike lightness, like a sheet of tissue paper, he slipped off—and tiptoed along the sticky, clinging—to the corner from which it seemed—it seemed to be—but coming closer, he realized that he was mistaken— the tapping was more to the right and higher up; he moved, and again got confused, fooled by the aural deception that occurs when a sound, traversing diagonally one's head, is hurriedly served by the wrong ear.

Stepping awkwardly, Cincinnatus brushed against the tray, which was standing on the floor near the wall. "Cincinnatus!" said the tray reproachfully; and then the tapping ceased with abrupt suddenness, which conveyed to the listener a heartening rationality; and, standing motionless by the wall, pressing down with his toe the spoon on the tray and tilting his open, hollow head, Cincinnatus felt that the unknown digger was also standing still and listening.

A half-minute passed and the sounds, quieter, more restrained, but more expressive and wiser, began again. Turning and slowly moving his sole off the zinc, Cincinnatus tried again to ascertain their location: to the right, if one stood facing the door ... yes, to the right, and, in any case, still far off ... after listening a long time that was all he was able to conclude. Finally moving back toward the cot to get his slippers—he could not stand it barefoot any longer—he startled the loud-legged chair, which never spent the night in the same spot twice, and again the sounds ceased, this time for good; that is, they might have resumed after a cautious interval, but morning was already coming into its own and Cincinnatus saw—with the eyes of habitual imagination—Rodion, all steaming from the dampness and opening in a yawn his bright-red mouth as he stretched on his stool in the hall.

All morning long Cincinnatus listened and calculated how he could make known his attitude to the sounds in case they should recur. A summer thunderstorm, simply yet tastefully staged, was performed outside: it was as dark as evening in the cell, thunder was heard, now substantial and round, now sharp and crackly, and lightning printed the shadows of the bars in unexpected places. At noon Rodrig Ivanovich arrived.

"You have company," he said, "but first I wanted to find out ..."

"Who?" asked Cincinnatus, at the same time thinking: please, not now ... (that is, please do not let the tapping resume now).

"You see, here's the way it is," said the director, "I am not sure that you wish ... You see, it's your mother—*votre mère, paraît-il.*"

"My mother?" asked Cincinnatus.

"Well, yes—mother, mummy, mama—in short, the

woman who gave birth to you. Shall I admit her? Make
up your mind quickly."

"... I have only seen her once in my life," said Cincinnatus, "and I really have no feeling ... no, no, it's not worth
it, don't, it would be pointless."

"As you wish," said the director and went out.

A minute later, cooing politely, he led in diminutive
Cecilia C., clad in a black raincoat. "I shall leave you two
alone," he added benevolently, "even though it is against
our rules, sometimes there are situations ... exceptions ...
mother and son ... I defer ..."

Exit, backing out like a courtier.

In her shiny black raincoat and a similar waterproof hat
with lowered brim (giving it something of the appearance
of a sou'wester), Cecilia C. remained standing in the center
of the cell, looking with a clear gaze at her son; she un-
buttoned herself; she sniffled noisily and said in her rapid,
choppy way: "What a storm, what mud, I thought I'd
never make it up here, streams and torrents coming down
the road at me ..."

"Sit down," said Cincinnatus, "don't stand like that."

"Say what you will, but it's quiet here in your place,"
she went on, sniffling all the while and rubbing her finger
firmly, as if it were a cheese grater, under her nose, so that
the pink tip wrinkled and wagged. "I'll say one thing, it's
quiet and fairly clean. By the way, over at the maternity
ward, we don't have private quarters as big as this. Oh, that
bed—my dear, just look what a mess your bed is!"

She plopped down her midwife's bag, nimbly pulled the
black cotton gloves off her small, mobile hands, and, stooping low over the cot, began making the bed afresh. Her

back in the belted coat with its seal-like sheen, her mended
stockings . . .

"Now, that's better," she said, straightening up; then,
standing for a moment with arms akimbo, she looked
askance at the book-cluttered table.

She was youthful, and all her features were a model for
those of Cincinnatus, which had emulated them in their
own way; Cincinnatus himself was vaguely aware of this resemblance as he looked at her sharp-nosed little face, and
protruding, luminous eyes. Her dress was opened in front,
revealing a triangle of red sun-tanned freckled skin; in general, however, the integument was the same as that from
which a piece had once been taken for Cincinnatus—a
pale, thin skin, with sky-blue veins.

"Tsk, tsk, a little straightening up would be in order here
too . . ." she prattled and, as quickly as she did everything
else, busied herself with the books, arranging them in even
piles. In passing her interest was caught by an illustration
in an open magazine; she fished out of her raincoat pocket
a kidney-shaped case and, dropping the corners of her
mouth, put on a pince-nez. "Came out back in '26," she
said with a laugh. "Such a long time ago, it's really hard to
believe it."

(Two photographs: in one the President of the Isles
shaking with a dental smile the hand of the venerable great
granddaughter of the last of the inventors at the Manches-
ter railroad station; in the other, a two-headed calf born in
a Danube village.)

She sighed causelessly, pushed the volume aside, knocked
the pencil off, did not catch it in time, and said "oops!"

"Leave as is," said Cincinnatus. "There can be no disorder here—only a shifting about."

"Here, I brought you this." (She pulled a pound bag out of her coat pocket, pulling out the lining as well.) "Here. Some candy. Suck on it to your heart's content."

She sat down and puffed out her cheeks.

"I climbed, and climbed, and finally made it, and now I am tired," she said, puffing deliberately; then she froze, gazing with vague longing at the cobweb up above.

"Why did you come?" asked Cincinnatus pacing about the cell. "It doesn't do you any good, and it doesn't do me any good. Why? It is neither kind, nor interesting. For I can see perfectly well that you are just as much of a parody as everybody and everything else. And if they treat me to such a clever parody of a mother . . . But imagine, for instance, that I have pinned my hopes on some distant sound —how can I have faith in it, if even *you* are a fraud? And you speak of 'candy!' Why not 'goodies'? And why is your raincoat wet when your shoes are dry—see, that's careless. Tell the prop man for me."

Hastily and guiltily, she said, "But I wore rubbers—I left them down in the office, word of honor."

"Oh, enough, enough. Just don't start explaining. Play your role—go heavy on the prattle and the unconcern— and you won't have to worry, it'll get by."

"I came because I am your mother," she said softly, and Cincinnatus burst out laughing:

"No, no, don't let it degenerate into farce. Remember, this is a drama. A little comedy is all right, but still you ought not to walk too far from the station—the drama might leave without you. You'd do better to . . . yes, I'll tell you what, why don't you tell me again the legend about my father. Can it be true that he vanished into the dark of night, and you never found out who he was or where he came from—it's strange . . ."

"Only his voice—I didn't see the face," she answered as softly as before.

"That's it, that's it, play up to me—I think perhaps we'll make him a runaway sailor," dejectedly continued Cincinnatus, snapping his fingers and pacing, pacing, "or a sylvan robber making a guest appearance in a public park. Or a wayward craftsman, a carpenter . . . Come, quickly, think of something."

"You don't understand," she cried (in her excitement she stood up and immediately sat down again). "It's true, I don't know who he was—a tramp, a fugitive, anything is possible . . . But why can't you understand . . . yes, it was a holiday, it was dark in the park, and I was still a child, but that's beside the point. The important thing is that it was not possible to make a mistake! A man who is being burned alive knows perfectly well that he isn't taking a dip in our Strop. Why, what I mean is, one can't be wrong . . . Oh, can't you understand?"

"Can't understand what?"

"Oh, Cincinnatus, he too was . . ."

"What do you mean, 'he too'?"

"He was also like you, Cincinnatus. . . ."

She quite lowered her face, dropping her pince-nez into her cupped hand.

Pause.

"How do you know this?" Cincinnatus asked morosely. "How can you suddenly notice . . ."

"I am not going to tell you anything more," she said without raising her eyes.

Cincinnatus sat down on the cot and lapsed into thought. His mother blew her nose with an extraordinarily loud trumpet sound, which one would hardly expect from so small a woman, and looked up at the window recess. Evidently the weather had cleared, for one felt the close presence of blue skies, and the sun had painted its stripe on the wall—now it would pale, then brighten again.

"There are cornflowers now in the rye," she said, speaking fast, "and everything is so wonderful—clouds are scudding, everything is so restless and bright. I live far from here, in Doctorton, and when I come to this city of yours, when I drive across the fields in the little old gig, and see the Strop gleaming, and this hill with the fortress on it, and everything, it always seems to me that a marvelous tale is being repeated over and over again, and I either don't have the time to, or am unable to grasp it, and still somebody keeps repeating it to me, with such patience! I work all day at our ward, I take everything in my stride, I have lovers, I adore ice-cold lemonade, although I've dropped smoking, because of heart trouble—and here I am sitting with you . . . I sit here and I don't know why I sit, why I bawl, and why I tell you all this, and now I shall be hot trudging down in this coat and this wool dress, the sun will be absolutely fiendish after a storm like that . . ."

"No, you're still only a parody," murmured Cincinnatus.

She smiled interrogatively.

"Just like this spider, just like those bars, just like the striking of that clock," murmured Cincinnatus.

"So," she said, and blew her nose again.

"So, that's how it is," she repeated.

They both remained silent, not looking at each other, while the clock struck with nonsensical resonance.

"When you go out," said Cincinnatus, "note the clock in the corridor. The dial is blank; however, every hour the watchman washes off the old hand and daubs on a new one—and that's how we live, by tarbrush time, and the ringing is the work of the watchman, which is why he is called a 'watch' man."

"You oughtn't joke like that," said Cecilia C. "There are, you know, all sorts of marvelous gimmicks. I remember, for instance when I was a child, there were objects called '*nonnons*' that were popular, and not only among children, but among adults too, and, you see, a special mirror came with them, not just crooked, but completely distorted. You couldn't make out anything of it, it was all gaps and jumble, and made no sense to the eye—yet the crookedness was no ordinary one, but calculated in just such a way as to . . . Or rather, to match its crookedness they had made . . . No, wait a minute, I am explaining badly. Well, you would have a crazy mirror like that and a whole collection of different '*nonnons*,' absolutely absurd objects, shapeless, mottled, pockmarked, knobby things, like some kind of fossils—but the mirror, which completely distorted ordinary objects, now, you see, got real food, that is, when you placed one of these incomprehensible, monstrous objects so that it was reflected in the incomprehensible, monstrous mirror, a marvelous thing happened; minus by minus equaled plus, everything was restored, everything was fine, and the shapeless speckledness became in the mirror a wonderful, sensible image; flowers, a ship, a person, a landscape. You could have your own portrait custom made, that is, you received some nightmarish jumble, and this thing was you, only the key to you was held by the mirror. Oh, I remember what fun it was, and how it was a little frightening—what if suddenly nothing should come out?—to pick up a new, incomprehensible '*nonnon*' and bring it near the mirror, and see your hand get all scrambled, and and at the same time see the meaningless '*nonnon*' turn into a charming picture, so very, very clear . . ."

"Why do you tell me all this?" asked Cincinnatus.

She was silent.

"What's the point of all this? Don't you know that one of these days, perhaps tomorrow . . ."

He suddenly noticed the expression in Cecilia C.'s eyes—just for an instant, an instant—but it was as if something real, unquestionable (in this world, where everything was subject to question), had passed through, as if a corner of this horrible life had curled up, and there was a glimpse of the lining. In his mother's gaze, Cincinnatus suddenly saw that ultimate, secure, all-explaining and from-all-protecting spark that he knew how to discern in himself also. What was this spark so piercingly expressing now? It does not matter what—call it horror, or pity . . . But rather let us say this: the spark proclaimed such a tumult of truth that Cincinnatus's soul could not help leaping for joy. The instant flashed and was gone. Cecilia C. got up, making an incredible little gesture, namely, holding her hands apart with index fingers extended, as if indicating size—the length, say, of a babe . . . Then she immediately began fussing, picking up from the floor her plump black bag, adjusting the lining of her pocket.

"There now," she said, in her former prattling tone, "I've stayed a while and now I'll be going. Eat my candy. I've overstayed. I'll be going, it's time."

"Oh yes, it's time!" thundered Rodrig Ivanovich with fierce mirth as he flung open the door.

Head bent, she slipped out. Cincinnatus, trembling, was about to step forward . . .

"Have no worry," said the director, raising his palm, "This little midwife presents no danger to us. Back!"

"But I would still . . ." began Cincinnatus.

"*Arrière!*" roared Rodrig Ivanovich.

Meanwhile, M'sieur Pierre's compact striped little figure appeared in the depths of the corridor. He was smiling pleasantly from afar, but restraining his pace slightly, and letting his eyes roam about furtively, as people do when they have walked in on a row, but do not want to stress their awareness of it. He was carrying a checkerboard and a box before him and had a punchinello doll and something else under his arm.

"You've had company?" he inquired politely of Cincinnatus when the director had left them alone in the cell. "Your mama visited you? That's fine, that's fine. And now I, poor, weak little M'sieur Pierre, have come to amuse you and amuse myself for a while. Just see how my Punch looks at you. Say hello to uncle. Isn't he a scream? Sit up, there, chum. Look, I've brought you lots of entertaining things. Would you like a game of chess first? Or cards? Do you play anchors? Splendid game! Come, I'll teach you!"

Thirteen

He waited and waited, and now, at last, in the stillest hour of night, the sounds got busy once again. Alone in the dark, Cincinnatus smiled. I am quite willing to admit that they are also a deception but right now I believe in them so much that I infect them with truth.

They were still more firm and precise than the previous night; they no longer were hacking away blindly; how could one doubt their approaching, advancing movement? How modest they were! How intelligent! How mysteriously calculating and insistent! Was it an ordinary pick or some outlandish implement made of some useless substance alloyed with omnipotent human will—but whatever it was, he knew that someone, somehow, was cutting a passage.

The night was cold; the gray, greasy reflection of the moon, dividing itself into squares, fell on the inner wall of the window recess; the whole fortress seemed to be filled to the brim with thick darkness on the inside, and glazed by the moonlight on the outside, with black broken shadows that slithered down rocky slopes and silently tumbled into the moats; yes, the night was impassive and stony—but within it, in its deep, dark womb, undermining its might, something was hacking its way through that was quite foreign to the night's substance and order. Or is this all but obsolete romantic rot, Cincinnatus?

He picked up the submissive chair and brought it down hard, first on the floor, then several times on the wall, trying, at least by means of rhythm, to impart meaning to his pounding. And, in fact, the one who was tunneling through the night first paused, as if trying to decide whether the answering blows were friendly or not, and suddenly renewed his labors with such a jubilantly animated sound that Cincinnatus was certain his response had been understood.

He was now satisfied that it was he to whom that someone was coming, that it was he whom that someone wanted to rescue, and, continuing to knock on the more sensitive sections of the stone, he evoked—in a different register and key, fuller, more complex, more enchanting—repetitions of the simple rhythms that he offered.

He was already thinking of how to set up an alphabet when he noticed that not the moon but a different, uninvited light was diluting the darkness, and he had barely noticed this when the sounds ceased. For quite a while afterwards there was a crumbling sound, but gradually this also grew silent, and it was hard to imagine that such a short time ago the stillness of night was being invaded by ardent, persistent activity, by a creature, sniffing, wheezing, with flattened muzzle, and again digging in frenzy, like a hound tunneling his way to a badger.

Through his brittle drowsiness he saw Rodion entering; and it was already past noon when he awoke fully, and thought, as always, that the end was not yet today, and it could have been today, just as easily as it might be tomorrow, but tomorrow was still far away.

All day long he harked to the humming in his ears, kneading his hands, as though silently exchanging with his own self a welcoming grip; he walked around the table, where the letter lay, still unsent; or else he would imagine the glance of yesterday's guest, momentary, breathtaking, like a hiatus in this life; or he would listen in fancy to Emmie's rustling movements. Well, why not drink this mush of hope, this thick, sweet slop . . . my hopes are still alive . . . and I thought that at least now, at least here, where solitude is held in such high esteem, it might divide into two parts only, for you and for me, instead of multiplying as it did—noisy, manifold, absurd, so that I could not even come near you, and your terrible father nearly broke my legs with his cane . . . this is why I am writing—this is my last attempt to explain to you what is happening, Marthe . . . make an exceptional effort and understand, if only through a fog, if only with a corner of your brain, but understand what is happening, Marthe, understand that they are going to kill me—can it be so difficult—I do not ask lengthy widow's lamentations from you, or mourning lilies, but implore you, I need it so badly—now,

today—just grow afraid like a child that they are going
to do something terrible to me, a vile thing that makes
you sick, and you scream so in the middle of the night
that even when you already hear nurse approaching, with
her "hush, hush," you still keep on screaming, that is
how you must be afraid, Marthe, even though you love
me little, you must still understand, even if only for an
instant, and then you may forget again. How can I stir
you? Oh, our life together was horrible, horrible, but I
cannot stir you with that, I tried hard at first, but, you
know, our tempos were different, and I immediately fell
behind. Tell me, how many hands have palpated the pulp
that has grown so generously around your hard, bitter little
soul? Yes, like a ghost I return to your first betrayals and,
howling, rattling my chains, walk through them. The kisses
I spied. Your and his kisses, which most resembled some
sort of feeding, intent, untidy, and noisy. Or when you,
with eyes closed tight, devoured a spurting peach and then,
having finished, but still swallowing, with your mouth still
full, you cannibal, your glazed eyes wandered, your fingers
were spread, your inflamed lips were all glossy, your chin
trembled, all covered with drops of the cloudy juice, which
trickled down onto your bared bosom, while the Priapus
who had nourished you suddenly, with a convulsive oath,
turned his bent back to me, who had entered the room at
the wrong moment. "All kinds of fruit are good for
Marthe," you would say with a certain sweet-slushy moist-
ness in your throat, all gathering into one damp, sweet,
accursed little fold—and if I return to all of this, it is to
get it out of my system, to purge myself—and also so that
you will know, so that you will know ... What? Probably

I am mistaking you for someone else, after all, when I
think that you will understand me, as an insane man mis-
takes his visiting kin for galaxies, logarithms, low-haunched
hyenas—but there are also madmen—and they are invulnerable—who take themselves for madmen—and here the
circle closes. Marthe, in some such circle you and I revolve
—oh, if only you could break away for an instant!—then
you can go back to it, I promise you . . . I do not ask a
great deal of you, only break away for an instant and
understand that they are murdering me, that we are surrounded by dummies, and that you are a dummy yourself.
I do not know why I was so tormented by your betrayals,
rather I myself know why, but I do not know the words
I must choose to make you understand why I was so tormented. Such words do not come in the small size that fits
your everyday needs. And yet I shall try again: "they are
murdering me!"—all right, all together once more: "they
are murdering me!"—and again: "murdering!". . . I want
to write this in such a way that you will cover your ears,
your membranaceous, simian ears that you hide under
strands of beautiful feminine hair—but I know them, I see
them, I pinch them, the cold little things, I worry them
with my fingers to somehow warm them, bring them to life,
render them human, force them to hear me. Marthe I want
you to obtain another interview, and, of course, come
alone, come alone! So-called life is finished for me, before
me there is only the polished block, and my jailers have
managed to drive me to such a state that my handwriting—
see—is like a drunken man's—but it does not matter, I
shall have strength enough, Marthe, for such a talk with
you as we have never yet had, that is why it is so necessary

that you come again, and do not think that this letter is a forgery—it is I, Cincinnatus, who am writing, it is I, Cincinnatus, who am weeping; and who was, in fact, walking around the table, and then, when Rodion brought his dinner, said:

"This letter. This letter I shall ask you to . . . Here is the address . . ."

"You'd do better to learn to knit like everybody else," grumbled Rodion, "so you could knit me a cache-knee. Writer, indeed! You just saw your missus, didn't you?"

"I shall try to ask you anyway," said Cincinnatus, "are there, besides me and that rather obtrusive Pierre, any other prisoners here?"

Rodion flushed but remained silent.

"And the headsman hasn't arrived yet?" asked Cincinnatus.

Rodion was about to furiously slam the already screeching door, but, as the day before, there entered, morocco slippers squeaking stickily, striped jelly-body quivering, hands carrying a chess set, cards, a cup-and-ball game—

"My humblest respects to friend Rodion," said M'sieur Pierre, in his reedy voice, and, without breaking stride, quivering, squeaking, he walked into the cell.

"I see," he said, seating himself, "that the dear fellow took a letter with him. Must have been the one that was lying here on the table yesterday, eh? To your spouse? No, no, a simple deduction, I don't read other people's letters, although it's true it was lying right in plain sight, while we were going at our game of anchors. How about some chess today?"

He spread out a checkerboard made of wool and with

his plump hand, cocking the little finger, he set up the places, which were fashioned of kneaded bread, according to an old prisoner's recipe, so solidly, that a stone might envy them.

"I'm a bachelor myself, but of course I understand . . . Forward. I shall quickly . . . Good players do not take a long time to think. Forward. I caught just a glimpse of your spouse—a juicy little piece, no two ways about it—what a neck, that's what I like . . . Hey, wait a minute, that was an oversight, allow me to take my move back. Here, this is better. I am a great aficionado of women, and the way they love me, the rascals, you simply wouldn't believe it. You were writing to your spouse there about her pretty eyes and lips. Recently, you know, I had . . . Why can't my pawn take it? Oh, I see. Clever, clever. All right, I retreat. Recently I had sexual intercourse with an extraordinarily healthy and splendid individual. What pleasure you experience, when a large brunette . . . What is this? That's a snide move on your part. You must warn your opponent, this won't do. Here, let me change my last move. So. Yes, a gorgeous, passionate creature—and, you know, I'm no piker myself, I've got such a spring that—wow! Generally speaking, of the numerous earthly temptations, which, in jest, but really with the utmost seriousness, I intend to submit gradually for your consideration, the temptation of sex . . . No, wait a minute, I haven't decided yet if I want to move that piece there. Yes, I will. What do you mean, checkmate? Why checkmate? I can't go here; I can't go there; I can't go anywhere. Wait a minute, what was the position? No, before that. Ah, now that's a different story. A mere oversight. All right, I'll move here. Yes, a red rose

between her teeth, black net stockings up to here, and not-a-stitch besides—that's really something, that's the supreme
... and now, instead of the raptures of love, dank stone, rusty iron, and ahead—well, you know yourself what lies ahead. Now this I overlooked. And what if I move other-wise? Yes, this is better. The game is mine, anyway—you make one mistake after another. What if she *was* unfaithful to you—didn't you also hold her in your embraces? When people ask me for advice I always tell them, 'Gentlemen, be inventive. There is nothing more pleasant, for example, than to surround oneself with mirrors and watch the good work going on there—wonderful! Hey! Now this is far from wonderful. Word of honor, I thought I had moved to this square, not to that. So therefore you were unable ... Back, please. Simultaneously I like to smoke a cigar and talk of insignificant matters, and I like her to talk too—there's nothing to be done, I have a certain streak of perversion in me ... Yes, how grievous, how frightening and hurtful to say farewell to all this—and to think that others, who are just as young and sappy, will continue to work and work ... ah! I don't know about you, but when it comes to caresses I love what we French wrestlers call '*macarons*': You give her a nice slap on the neck, and, the firmer the meat ... First of all, I can take your knight, secondly, I can simply move my king away; all right—there. No, stop, stop, I'd like to think for a minute after all. What was your last move? Put that piece back and let me think. Nonsense, there's no checkmate here. You, it seems to me—if you do not mind my saying so—are cheating: this piece stood here, or maybe here, but not there, I am absolutely certain. Come, put it back, put it back ..."

As though accidentally, he knocked over several men, and, unable to restrain himself, with a groan, he mixed up the remainder. Cincinnatus sat leaning on one elbow; he was pensively picking at a knight which, in the neck region, seemed not loath to return to the mealy state whence it had sprung.

"Let's start some other game, you don't know how to play chess," fussily cried M'sieur Pierre and opened up a varicolored board for "goose." He cast the dice, and immediately climbed from 3 to 27—although then he had to come back down while Cincinnatus zoomed from 22 to 46. The game dragged on for a long time. M'sieur Pierre would grow purple, stamp his feet, fume, crawl under the table after the dice and emerge holding them in his palm and swearing that that was exactly the way they had been lying on the floor.

"Why do you smell like that?" asked Cincinnatus with a sigh. M'sieur Pierre's plump face twisted into a forced smile.

"It runs in the family," he explained with dignity. "Feet sweat a little. I've tried alums, but nothing works. I must say that, although I have been afflicted with this since childhood, and although any suffering is customarily regarded with respect, no one has ever yet been so tactless . . ."

"I can't breathe," said Cincinnatus.

Fourteen

The sounds were still closer, and now they hurried so that it would have been a sin to distract them by tapping out questions. And they continued later than the night before, and Cincinatus lay prone on the flagstones, spread-eagled as one who has been felled by a sunstroke, and indulging the mummery of the senses, clearly visualized through the tympanum the secret passage, lengthening with every scrape, and sensed—as if thus the dark, tight pain in his chest were relieved—how the stones were being loosened, and he had already begun guessing, as he looked at the wall, where it would crack and burst open with a crash.

Crackling and rustling noises were still audible when Rodion came in. Behind him, in ballet shoes on her bare feet and a tartan dress, Emmie darted in and, as she had done once before, hid under the table, crouching there on her haunches, so that her flaxen hair, curling at the tips, covered her face and her knees, and even her ankles. Barely had Rodion gone when she sprang up and went straight to Cincinnatus, who was sitting on the cot, and, overturning him, began scrambling all over him. Her cold fingers and hot elbows dug into him, she bared her teeth, a fragment of green leaf had stuck to her front teeth.

"Sit still," said Cincinnatus, "I'm exhausted—I didn't weep a slink all night—sit still and tell me . . ."

Fidgeting, Emmie buried her forehead in his chest; her curls tumbling and hanging to one side, revealed the bare upper part of her back, which had a hollow that moved with her shoulder blades and was evenly covered with a blond down, which looked as though it had been combed in a symmetrical pattern.

Cincinnatus stroked her warm head, trying to raise it. She snatched his fingers and began pressing them to her quick lips.

"What a snuggling pet you are," said Cincinnatus drowsily. "That will do, enough now. Tell me . . ."

But she was seized by an outburst of childish boisterousness. The muscular child rolled Cincinnatus about like a puppy. "Stop it!" cried Cincinnatus. "Aren't you ashamed of yourself?"

"Tomorrow," she said suddenly, squeezing him and gazing at him between the eyes.

"Tomorrow I'll die?" asked Cincinnatus.

"No, I'll rescue you," Emmie said pensively (she was seated astride him).

"That's very nice indeed," said Cincinnatus. "Saviors from all sides! This ought to have happened sooner—I'm nearly insane. Please get off, you are heavy and hot."

"We'll run away and you'll marry me."

"Maybe when you are a little older; only I already have one wife."

"A fat, old one," said Emmie.

She hopped off the cot and ran around the room, as ballerinas run, at a fast striding pace, shaking her hair, and then she leaped, as though flying, and finally pirouetted in one spot, flinging out a multitude of arms.

"School will be starting again soon," she said, settling the next moment on Cincinnatus's lap; suddenly, forgetting everything else in the world, she became engrossed in a new occupation—she began picking at a black lengthwise scab on her shiny shin; the scab was already half off, and one could see the tender pink scar.

Through slitted eyes, Cincinnatus gazed at her inclined profile, rimmed with a bloom of sunlight, and he felt suffused with drowsiness.

"Ah, Emmie, remember, remember what you have promised. Tomorrow! Tell me, how will you do it?"

"Give me your ear," said Emmie.

Putting one arm around his neck, she made a hot, moist and utterly unintelligible noise in his ear. "I can't hear anything," said Cincinnatus.

Impatiently she brushed the hair back from her face and again nestled up to him.

"Bu . . . bu . . . bu," she bumbled and buzzed—and then jumped away, and flew up—and now was resting on the slightly swaying trapeze, her extended toes joined in a sharp wedge.

"Still, I'm counting on this very much," said Cincinnatus through mounting sleepiness; slowly he pressed his wet, singing ear to the pillow.

As he was falling asleep he could feel her climbing over him, and then it seemed dimly to him that she or someone else was endlessly folding some shiny fabric, taking it by the corners and folding, and stroking it with the palm, and folding it again—and for a moment he came to from Emmie's squeal as Rodion dragged her out of the cell.

Then he thought he heard the precious sounds behind the wall start cautiously again . . . how risky! After all, it was broad daylight . . . but they could not restrain themselves, and ever so quietly pushed closer and closer to him, while he, fearing lest the guards hear, began walking about, stamping his feet, coughing, humming, and when, with a violently beating heart, he sat down at the table, the sounds had already ceased.

Then, toward evening, as was now customary, M'sieur Pierre arrived, in a brocade skullcap; casually, being quite at home, he lay down on Cincinnatus's cot and, lighting a long meerschaum pipe with a carved houri, propped himself up on an elbow in a cloud of luxurious smoke. Cincinnatus sat at the table, munching the last of his supper, fishing the prunes out of their brown juice.

"I put some foot powder on them today," M'sieur Pierre said briskly, "So no complaints or comments, please. Let us continue our conversation of yesterday. We were talking of pleasures.

"The pleasure of love," said M'sieur Pierre, "is achieved by means of the most beautiful and healthful of all known physical exercises. I said 'achieved' but perhaps 'extracted' would be even more apt, inasmuch as we are dealing precisely with a systematic and persistent extraction of pleasure buried in the very bowels of the belabored creature. During leisure hours the laborer of love immediately strikes the observer with the falconlike expression of his eyes, his cheerful disposition, and his fresh complexion. Observe also my gliding gait. Thus we have before us a certain phenomenon, which we may call by the general term 'love' or 'erotic pleasure.' "

At this point, walking on tiptoe and indicating by gestures that they should not pay him any notice, the director came in and sat down on a stool that he himself had brought.

M'sieur Pierre turned on him a gaze beaming with benevolence.

"Go on, go on," whispered Rodrig Ivanovich, "I've come to listen—*pardon*, just one moment—I'll just put it so I can lean against the wall. *Voilà.* I'm worn out, though. And you?"

"That's because you are not used to it," said M'sieur Pierre. "Allow me, then, to continue. We were discussing, Rodrig Ivanovich, the pleasures of life, and had just examined Eros in a general way."

"I see," said the director.

"I made the following points—excuse me, dear colleague, for repeating myself, but I would like to make it interesting for Rodrig Ivanovich also. I made the point, Rodrig Ivanovich, that a man condemned to die finds it hardest of all to forget woman, woman's delicious body."

"And the poetry of moonlit nights," added Rodrig Ivano-vich, casting a stern glance at Cincinnatus.

"No, please don't interfere with my development of the subject; if you have something to add, you may do so afterwards. All right—let me continue. In addition to the pleasures of love there is a whole number of others, and to them we shall now pass on. More than once, probably, you have felt your chest expand on a wonderful spring day, when the buds swell and feathered songsters enliven the groves, clad in their first sticky leafage. The first modest flowers peep coquettishly out of the grass, as if they would entice the passionate lover of nature, as they whisper timidly: 'Oh, don't, don't pick us, our life is short.' The chest expands and breathes deep on such a day, when the birdies sing, and the first modest leaves appear on the first trees. Everything rejoices, everything is jubilant."

"A masterful description of April," said the director, giving his jowls a shake.

"I think that everyone has experienced this," continued M'sieur Pierre, "and now, when any day now we shall all be ascending the scaffold, the unforgettable memory of such a spring day makes one cry out: 'O come back, come back; let me live you over once again.' "

" 'Live you over once again,' " repeated M'sieur Pierre, rather frankly consulting a scroll-like crib, all covered with fine writing.

"Next," said M'sieur Pierre, "we pass on to pleasures of a spiritual order. Remember the times when, in a fabulous picture gallery, or museum, you would suddenly stop and be unable to take your eyes off some piquant torso—made, alas, of bronze or marble. This we can call the pleasure of art; it occupies an important place in life."

"I'll say it does," said Rodrig Ivanovich in a nasal voice, and looked at Cincinnatus.

"Gastronomic pleasures," continued M'sieur Pierre. "See the best varieties of fruit hanging from tree branches; see the butcher and his helpers dragging a pig, squealing as if it were being slaughtered; see, on a pretty plate, a substantial chunk of white lard; see the table wine and cherry brandy; see the fish—I don't know about the rest of you, but I am a great fancier of bream."

"I approve," Rodrig Ivanovich said resonantly.

"This splendid feast must be forsaken. Many other things must be forsaken as well: festive music, favorite knick-knacks, such as a camera or a pipe; friendly talks; the bliss of relieving oneself, which some hold to be on a par with the pleasure of love; sleep after dinner; smoking . . . What else? Favorite knick-knacks . . . Yes, we already had that" (again the crib notes appeared) "pleasure . . . I've said that too. Well, various other trifles . . ."

"May I add something," the director asked ingratiatingly, but M'sieur Pierre shook his head:

"No, that's quite enough. I think I have unfolded before the mental eye of my dear colleague such vistas of sensual realms . . ."

"I only wanted to say something on the subject of edibles," the director remarked in a low voice. "I think certain details could be mentioned here. For instance, *en fait de potage* . . . All right, all right, I shan't say a word," he concluded in alarm as he met the gaze of M'sieur Pierre.

"Well," M'sieur Pierre addressed Cincinnatus, "what will you say to all this?"

"What am I supposed to say?" said Cincinnatus. "Dreary, obtrusive nonsense."

"He's incorrigible," exclaimed Rodrig Ivanovich.

"It's just a pose on his part," said M'sieur Pierre with an ominous porcelain smile. "Believe me, he has feeling enough for the full beauty of the phenomena I have described."

". . . But fails to understand certain things," Rodrig Ivanovich interjected smoothly. "He does not understand that if he were now honestly to admit the error of his ways, honestly admit that he is fond of the same things as you and I—for example, turtle soup for the first course—they say it's sensationally good—that is, I only want to observe that if he were honestly to admit and repent—yes, repent—that is my point—then he could have some remote—I do not want to say hope, but nevertheless . . ."

"I left out the part about gymnastics," muttered M'sieur Pierre checking his little scroll. "What a pity!"

"No, no, you spoke very well, very well," sighed Rodrig Ivanovich. "Couldn't be better. You roused in me certain desires that had lain dormant for decades. Will you stay a while? Or are you coming with me?"

"With you. He's a regular sourpuss today. Doesn't even look at you. You offer him kingdoms, and he sulks. And I ask so little—one word, a nod. Well, nothing to be done. Let's away, Rodrigo."

Soon after their departure the light went out and Cincinnatus transferred himself to his cot in darkness (how nasty to find somebody else's ashes, but no other place to lie down) and, liberating his melancholy in a crackling of cartileges and vertebrae, he stretched, and drew in a breath, and held it a quarter of a minute and more. Maybe it was just stonemasons. Making repairs. An aural deception: perhaps it is all going on far, far away (he exhaled). He lay on his back, wriggling his toes, which protruded from beneath the blanket and turning his face now toward impossible salvation, now toward inevitable execution. The light flashed on again.

Scratching at the red-haired chest under his shirt, Rodion arrived to fetch the stool. Seeing the object he sought, he promptly sat down on it and with a loud grunt, kneaded his lowered face with his enormous palm, and apparently got ready to have a nap.

"He still has not arrived?" asked Cincinnatus.

Rodion immediately got up and left with the stool.

Click. Black.

Perhaps because a certain integral period of time—a fortnight—had elapsed since the trial, perhaps because the nearing of the friendly sounds promised him a change of fortune, Cincinnatus spent this night in a mental review of the hours he had passed in the fortress. Involuntarily yielding to the temptation of logical development, involuntarily (be careful, Cincinnatus!) forging into a chain all the things that were quite harmless as long as they remained unlinked, he inspired the meaningless with meaning, and the lifeless with life. With the stone darkness for background he now permitted the spotlighted figures of all his usual visitors to appear—it was the very first time that his imagination was so condescending toward them. There was the tiresome little co-prisoner, with his shiny face, resembling the wax apple which Cincinnatus's waggish brother-in-law had brought the other day; there was the fidgety, lean lawyer, disengaging his shirt cuffs from the sleeves of his frock coat; there was the somber librarian, and, in smooth black toupee, corpulent Rodrig Ivanovich, and Emmie, and Marthe's entire family, and Rodion, and others, vague guards and soldiers—and by evoking them—not believing in them, perhaps, but still evoking them—Cincinnatus allowed them the right to exist, supported them, nourished them with himself. Added to all this was the possibility that, at any moment, the exciting knocks might resume, a possibility that had the effect of an intoxicating anticipation of music—so that Cincinnatus was in a strange, tremulous, dangerous state—and the distant clock struck with a kind of mounting exultation—and now, emerging from the darkness, the lighted figures joined hands and formed a ring—and, slightly swaying to one side, lurching, lagging, they began a circling movement, which at first was stiff and dragging, but then gradually became more even, free and rapid, and now they were whirling in earnest, and the monstrous shadow of their shoulders and heads passed and repassed ever more quickly across the stone vaults, and the inevitable joker who, when whirling in a reel, kicks his legs high, to amuse his more prim companions, cast on the walls the huge black zigzags of his hideous prance.

Fifteen

The morning passed quietly, but at about five in the afternoon there started a noise of shattering force: whoever it was he worked furiously and clattered shamelessly; actually however, he had not come much nearer since yesterday.

Suddenly an extraordinary thing happened: some inner obstruction collapsed, and now the noises sounded with such vivid intensity (having in an instant made the transition from background to foreground, right up to the footlights) that their proximity was obvious: they were right there, directly behind the wall, which was melting like ice, and would break through it any instant now.

And then the prisoner decided that it was time to act.

With terrible haste, trembling, but still trying to keep control over himself, he got out and put on the rubber shoes, the linen trousers and the jacket he had been wearing when arrested; he found a handkerchief, two handkerchiefs, three handkerchiefs (a fleeting vision of sheets tied together); just in case, he put in his pocket a chance piece of string with a wooden handle for carrying packages still attached (it wouldn't go in completely—the end remained hanging out); he rushed to the bed, intending to fluff up the pillow and cover it with the blanket in such a way as to create the semblance of a sleeping man; he did not do this, but lunged instead to the table with the intention of taking along what he had written; but here also he changed direction at the halfway point, for the triumphant, mad, pounding noises were confusing his thoughts . . . He was standing straight as an arrow, his hands at his seams, when, in perfect fulfillment of his dreams, the yellow wall cracked about a yard above the floor in a lightninglike pattern, immediately bulged from the pressure within, and suddenly burst open with a great crash.

Out of the black hole, in a cloud of debris, pick in hand, all dusted with white, twisting and threshing like a fat fish among the dust, and rippling with laughter, climbed M'sieur Pierre, and right behind him, but in crab fashion, fat backside first, revealing a tear from which a tuft of white cotton protruded, coatless, and also covered with all kinds of rubble, also splitting with mirth, came Rodrig Ivanovich. Having tumbled out of the hole, they both sat down on the floor and now shook with unrestrained laughter, with all the transitions from guffaw to chuckle and back again, with piteous squeals in the intervals between outbursts, all the while nudging each other, falling over each other ...

"It's us, it's us, it's us," M'sieur Pierre finally managed with an effort, turning his chalk-white face to Cincinnatus, while his little yellow wig rose with a comic whistle and settled again.

"It's us," said Rodrig Ivanovich in an unaccustomed falsetto and once again began to guffaw, flinging up his soft legs, clad in an *Auguste's* grotesque spats.

"Ooph!" said M'sieur Pierre, who had suddenly quieted down; he got up off the floor and, striking one palm against the other, looked back at the hole: "Quite a little job we've done, Rodrig Ivanovich! Come, get up, my fine friend, that's enough. What a job! Oh well, now we can make use of this splendid tunnel ... Allow me to invite you, dear neighbor, to come and have a glass of tea with me."

"If you so much as touch me ..." murmured Cincinnatus and, as on one side, white, sweaty M'sieur Pierre stood ready to embrace him and shove him in, and, on the other, stood Rodrig Ivanovich, also with open arms, bare-shouldered, and with dickey loose and awry, both of them gathering momentum before piling on him, Cincinnatus took the only possible direction, namely the one being indicated to him. M'sieur Pierre was nudging him lightly from behind, helping him crawl into the opening. "Join us," he said to Rodrig Ivanovich, but the latter declined, pleading disarray.

Flattened out and with eyes shut tight, Cincinnatus crawled on all fours, M'sieur Pierre crawled behind, and the pitch darkness, full of crumbling and crackling, squeezed Cincinnatus from all sides, pressed on his spine, prickled his palms and his knees; several times Cincinnatus found

himself in a cul-de-sac, and then M'sieur Pierre would tug
at his calves, making him back out of the dead end, and
every instant a corner, a protrusion, he knew not what,
would brush painfully against his head, and all in all he was
overcome by such terrible, unmitigated dejection that, had
there not been a wheezing, butting companion behind, he
would have lain down and died then and there. At last,
however, after they had been moving for a long time through
the narrow, coal-black darkness (in one place, off to the
side, a red lantern imparted a dull luster to the blackness),
after the closeness, the blindness, and the stuffiness, a pale
luminosity expanded in the distance: there was a bend
there, and finally came the exit; awkwardly and meekly
Cincinnatus fell out onto the stone floor, into M'sieur
Pierre's sun-drenched cell.

"Welcome," said his host, climbing out after him; he
promptly produced a clothesbrush and began skillfully
brushing off blinking Cincinnatus, considerately restraining
and softening the strokes in any area that might be sensitive.
As he did so he bent over and, as if enmeshing him in something, kept walking around Cincinnatus, who stood perfectly still, astounded by a certain extraordinarily simple
thought; astounded, rather, not by the thought but by the
fact that it had not come to him sooner.

"With your permission I'll change," spoke M'sieur Pierre
and pulled off his dusty sweater; for an instant, with sham
casualness, he flexed his arm, casting a sidelong glance at
his turquoise-and-white biceps and exuding his characteristic
stench. Around his left nipple there was an imaginative
tattoo—two green leaves—so that the nipple itself seemed to
be a rosebud (made of marchpane and candied angelica).

"Have a seat, please," he said, putting on a robe with bright arabesques. "It's all I have, but it's mine. My quarters, as you see, are almost exactly like yours. Only I keep them clean and decorate them . . . I decorate them as best I can." (He gasped slightly, as if from uncontrollable excitement.) I decorate. The wall calendar with the water color of the fortress at sunset exhibited a crimson numeral. A crazy-quilt blanket covered the cot. Above it, attached by thumbtacks, hung salacious photographs and a formal picture of M'sieur Pierre; a goffered paper fan stuck its crimped pleats from behind the edge of the frame. On the table lay an alligator-skin album, the face of a gold traveling clock glistened, and half a dozen velvety pansies looked out in various directions over the burnished rim of a porcelain mug bearing a German landscape. In a corner of the cell stood a large case containing possibly some musical instrument.

"I am exceedingly happy to see you here in my place," M'sieur Pierre was saying as he promenaded back and forth, passing each time through an oblique ray of sunlight in which plaster dust still danced. "I feel that in the past week we have become such good friends, have come together so well, so warmly, as seldom happens. I see you are interested to know what is inside. Just let me [he caught his breath], let me finish and then I shall show you . . ."

"Our friendship," continued M'sieur Pierre, pacing and gasping slightly, "has flowered in the hothouse-like atmosphere of a prison, where it was nourished by the same alarms and the same hopes. I think I know you better now than anyone else does in the whole world, and certainly more intimately than your wife knew you. Therefore I find it particularly painful when you give in to a feeling of

spite or are inconsiderate of people . . . Just now, for instance, when we came to you so joyously, you again insulted
Rodrig Ivanovich with your assumed indifference to the surprise in which he had taken part so kindly, so energetically
—and do not forget he is no longer young, and has many
troubles of his own. No, I would rather not talk about this
now . . . I only want to establish that not the slightest shade
of feeling on your part escapes me, and therefore I per-
sonally feel that the well-known accusation is not quite fair
. . . To me you are transparent as—excuse the sophisticated
simile—a blushing bride is transparent to the gaze of an experienced bridegroom. I don't know, there's something
wrong with my breathing—excuse me, it will pass in a moment. But, if I have made such a close study of you and—
why keep it a secret?—have grown fond, very fond of you,
then you also must needs have grown to know me, grown
accustomed to me—more than that, grown attached to me,
as I to you. To achieve such a friendship—that was my first
task, and it seems I have performed it successfully. Successfully. Now we are going to have tea. I can't understand
why they don't bring it."

Clutching at his chest, he sat down at the table across
from Cincinnatus but instantly sprang up again; from under
his pillow he produced a morocco purse, from the purse a
chamois sheath, and from the sheath a key; he went to the
large case that was standing in the corner.

"I see that you are amazed by my neatness," he said as
he carefully inclined the propped up case, which proved to
be heavy and cumbersome. "But you see, neatness adorns
the life of a lone bachelor, who thus proves to himself . . ."

He opened the case. There, upon black velvet, lay a broad, shiny ax.

". . . proves to himself that he does have a little nest . . . A little nest," M'sieur Pierre went on, locking the case again, leaning it against the wall, and himself leaning, "a little nest that he has deserved, built, filled with his warmth. . . . In general, there is an important philosophical theme here, but from certain indications it seems to me that you, as I, are not in the mood for themes just now. Do you know what? Here is my advice: we'll have our cup of tea later; right now, though, go back to your place and lie down for a while—yes, go. We are both young—you must not remain here any longer. Tomorrow they will explain to you, but now please go. I too am excited, I too am not in complete control of myself, you must understand this . . ."

Cincinnatus was quietly fiddling with the locked door.

"No, no—you use our tunnel. We didn't put in all this work for nothing. Crawl in, crawl in. I drape the hole, or else it would not look well. Go . . ."

"By myself," said Cincinnatus.

He climbed into the black opening, and hurting his knees anew, began to crawl on all fours, deeper and deeper into the narrow darkness. M'sieur Pierre yelled something after him about tea and then apparently drew the curtain, for Cincinnatus immediately felt cut off from the bright cell where he had just been.

Breathing the rough air with difficulty, running into sharp projections—and expecting, without especial fear, that the tunnel would collapse—Cincinnatus groped blindly through the winding passage, found himself in stone cul-de-sacs and, like some patient retreating animal, moved backwards; then, feeling out the tunnel's continuation, crawled on. He was impatient to lie down on something soft, even if it were only his cot, to pull the covers up over his head, and not think about anything. This return journey dragged out so that, skinning his shoulders, he began to hurry as much as the constant apprehension of a dead end would permit him. The closeness made him groggy, and he was just deciding to stop, to lie prone, to imagine that he was in bed and with this to go to sleep, when abruptly the surface along which he was crawling began to slope, and he glimpsed the gleam of a reddish chink ahead and caught a whiff of dampness and mold just as though he had passed from the bowels of the fortress wall into a natural cave, and from the low ceiling, muffled up bats, hanging like wrinkled fruit, awaited their cue, each holding on by a claw, head down; the chink opened in a blaze of light, and there was a breath of fresh evening air, and Cincinnatus crawled from a crack in the rock to freedom.

He found himself on one of the many turfy taluses which, like dark-green waves, lapped up sharply at various levels among the rocks and ramparts of the terraced fortress. At first he was so dizzy from liberty, altitude and space that he clutched at the damp turf and hardly noticed anything besides the loud evening cries of the swallows as they snipped the colored air with their black scissors; the glow of sunset had invaded half the sky; and, right behind his head, there swept up with awful swiftness the blind stone steeps of the fortress out of which he had oozed like a drop of water; while at his feet there were fantastic precipices and clover-scented mists.

He regained his breath and got used to the brightness

dazzling him, to the trembling of his body, to the impact of the freedom that reverberated afar and welled up within him. He glued his back to the rock and contemplated the hazy landscape. Far below, where twilight had already settled, he could barely discern through wisps of mist the ornate hump of the bridge. While yonder, on the other side, the blurred blue city, its windows like embers, was either still borrowing the sunset's blaze or else perhaps had lit up at its own expense; he could make out the gradual threading of the bright beads of street lights as they were being lit along Steep Avenue—and there was an exceptionally distinct, delicate arch at its upper end. Beyond the city everything shimmered dimly, merged, and dissolved; but, above the invisible Gardens, in the rosy depths of the sky, stood a chain of translucent and fiery cloudlets, and there stretched a long violet bank with burning rents along its lower edge—and while Cincinnatus gazed, yonder, yonder an oak-covered hill flashed with Venetian Green and slowly sank into shadow.

Intoxicated, weak, slipping on the coarse turf, and catching his balance, he set off downward, and immediately, from behind a projection of the rampart, where a black bramble bush rustled its warning, Emmie darted out to him, her face and legs painted pink by the sunset, and, firmly grasping him by the hand, dragged him after her. All her movements betrayed excitement, rapturous haste. "Where are we going? Down?" Cincinnatus inquired haltingly, laughing from impatience. She quickly led him along the fortress wall. A small green door opened in the wall. Stairs, leading down, passed imperceptibly underfoot. Again a door creaked; beyond it was a darkish passage in which stood trunks, a wardrobe, and a ladder resting against the wall, and there was a smell of kerosene; it was now apparent that they had entered the director's apartment by the back way for, now no longer clutching his fingers quite so tightly, already absent-mindedly releasing them, Emmie led him into a dining room where they were all sitting and drinking tea at a lighted oval table. Rodrig Ivanovich's napkin amply covered his chest; his wife—thin, freckled, with white eyelashes—was passing the pretzels to M'sieur Pierre, who had dressed up in a Russian shirt embroidered with cocks; balls of colored wool and glassy knitting needles lay in a basket by the samovar. A sharp-nosed little old crone in a mobcap and black shawl was hunched at one end of the table.

When he saw Cincinnatus the director gaped, and something drooled from one corner of his mouth.

"Pfui, you naughty child!" said the director's wife to Emmie with a slight German accent.

M'sieur Pierre, who was stirring his tea, demurely lowered his eyes.

"What's the meaning of this escapade?" Rodrig Ivanovich said through the trickling melon juice. "To say nothing of the fact that this is against all regulations!"

"Let them be," said M'sieur Pierre without raising his eyes. "After all, they are both children."

"It's the end of her vacation, so she wants to play a prank," put in the director's wife.

Emmie sat down at the table, deliberately making her chair scrape, fidgeting and wetting her lips and having dismissed Cincinnatus forever, began spreading sugar (which immediately assumed an orange hue) on her shaggy slice of melon; thereupon she bit into it busily, holding it by the ends, which reached her ears, and brushing her neighbor with her elbow. Her neighbor continued to sip his tea, holding the spoon protruding from it between second and third fingers, but inconspicuously, reached under the table with his left hand. "Eek!" cried Emmie as she gave a ticklish start, without, however, taking her mouth from the melon.

"Sit down over there for the time being," said the director, with his fruit knife indicating to Cincinnatus a green armchair with an antimacassar that stood aloof in the damask dusk near the folds of the window draperies. "When we finish I'll take you back. I said sit down. What's the matter with you? What's wrong with him? What a slow-witted fellow!"

M'sieur Pierre leaned over to Rodrig Ivanovich and, blushing slightly, imparted to him something.

The latter's larynx emitted a regular thunderclap:

"Well, congratulations, congratulations," he said, restraining with difficulty the gusts of his voice. "This *is* good news!—It's high time you informed him—We all . . ." He glanced at Cincinnatus and was about to launch on a formal—

"No, not yet, my friend, don't embarrass me," murmured M'sieur Pierre, touching his sleeve.

"In any case, you won't refuse another tumbler of tea," said Rodrig Ivanovich playfully, and then, after a moment of reflection and some champing, he addressed Cincinnatus.

"Hey, you there. You can look at the album meanwhile. Child, give him the album. For her" (gesture with the knife) "return to school our dear guest has made her—has made her a—Pardon me, Pyotr Petrovich, I've forgotten what you called it."

"A photohoroscope," M'sieur Pierre replied modestly.

"Shall I leave the lemon in?" asked the director's wife. The hanging kerosene lamp, whose light did not reach the back of the dining room (where only the gleam of a pendulum flashed as it hacked off the solid seconds) flooded the cozily spread table with a familial light, which graded into the chinking sounds of the tea ritual.

Sixteen

Let us be calm. The spider had sucked dry a small downy moth with marbled forewings, and three houseflies, but was still hungry and kept glancing at the door. Let us be calm. Cincinnatus was a mass of scrapes and bruises. Be calm; nothing had happened. Last night, when they brought him back to the cell, two employees were just finishing plastering the place where lately the hole had gaped. That place was now marked only by swirls of paint a bit rounder and thicker than elsewhere, and he had a stifling sensation whenever he glanced at the wall, which again was blind, deaf and impenetrable.

Another vestige of the previous day was the alligator album with its massive dark silver monogram that he had taken along in a fit of meek abstraction: that singular photo-horoscope put together by the resourceful M'sieur Pierre, that is, a series of photographs depicting the natural progression of a given person's entire life. How was this done? Thus: extensively retouched snapshots of Emmie's present face were supplemented by shots of other people—for the sake of costume, furniture and surroundings—so as to create the entire décor and stage properties of her future life. Consecutively stuck into the polygonal little windows of the solid, gilt-edged cardboard, and supplied with finely inscribed dates, these sharp and, at first sight, genuine photographs pictured Emmie first as she was at present; then at fourteen, an attaché case in her hand; then at sixteen, in tights and tutu, with gaseous wings growing from her back, seated relaxed on a table, and lifting a goblet of wine amid rakes; then, at eighteen, in *femme-fatale* weeds, at a railing above a waterfall; then ... oh, in many more aspects and poses, even to the very last, horizontal.

By means of retouching and other photographic tricks, what appeared to be progressive changes in Emmie's face had been achieved (incidentally, the trickster had made use of her mother's photographs); but one had only to look closer and it became repulsively obvious how trite was this parody of the work of time. The Emmie who was leaving by the stage door, in furs, with flowers pressed to her shoulder, had limbs that had never danced; while in the next shot, showing her already in her bridal veil, the groom at her side was tall and slender, but had the round little face of M'sieur Pierre. At thirty she already had what was supposed to look like wrinkles, drawn in without meaning, without life, without knowledge of their true significance, but conveying something very bizarre to the expert, as a chance stirring of a tree's branches may coincide with a sign gesture comprehensible to a deaf-mute. And at forty Emmie was dying—and here allow me to congratulate you on an inverse error: her face in death could never pass for the face of death!

Rodion bore this album away, mumbling that the young lady was just leaving, and when he next appeared he deemed it necessary to announce that the young lady had left:

(Sighing) "Gone, gone . . ." (To the spider) "Enough, you've had enough . . ." (Showing his palm) "I don't have anything for you." (To Cincinnatus again) "It'll be dull, so dull without our little daughter . . . how she flitted about, what music she made, our spoiled darling, our golden flower." (Pause. Then, in a different tone) "What's the matter, good sir, why don't you ask those catchy questions any more? Well? So, so," Rodion convincingly replied to himself and withdrew with dignity.

After dinner, quite formally, no longer in prison garb but in a velvet jacket, an arty bow tie and new, high-heeled, insinuatingly squeaking boots with glossy legs (making him somehow resemble an operatic woodman), M'sieur Pierre came in, and, behind him, respectfully yielding to him first place in perambulation, speech, everything, came Rodrig Ivanovich and the lawyer with his briefcase. The three of them settled themselves at the table in wicker chairs (brought from the waiting room), while Cincinnatus walked about the cell, in single combat with shameful fear; but presently he also sat down.

Somewhat clumsily (with a clumsiness that was, however, practiced and familiar) fussing with the briefcase, yanking open its black cheek, holding it partly on his knee, partly leaning it against the table—it would slip off one point, then off the other—the lawyer produced a large writing pad and locked, or rather buttoned up the briefcase, which yielded too readily and therefore at first muffed the fastening nip; he was just placing it on the table, but changed his mind and, taking it by the collar, lowered it to the floor, leaning it against a leg of his chair where it assumed the drooping position of a drunk; he then produced from his lapel an enameled pencil, on the back swing opened the pad and, paying attention to no one and nothing, began covering the detachable pages with even writing; however, this very inattention made all the more obvious the connection between the rapid movement of his pencil and the conference for which everyone had gathered here.

Rodrig Ivanovich was sitting in the easy chair, leaning back slightly, making the chair creak by the pressure of his solid back, with one purplish paw resting on the arm of his chair and the other thrust in the bosom of his frock coat; every once in a while he would jerk his flabby cheeks and his chin, powdered like a Turkish delight, as if freeing them from some viscous and absorbing element.

M'sieur Pierre, seated in the center, poured himself water from a decanter, then ever so carefully placed his hands, on the table, fingers interlaced (an artificial aquamarine flashing on his little finger) and, lowering his long eyelashes for ten seconds or so pondered reverently how he would begin his speech.

"Kind gentlemen," M'sieur Pierre finally said in a high voice, without raising his eyes, "first of all and before anything else, allow me to outline by means of a few deft strokes what has already been accomplished by me."

"Proceed, we beg you," said the director resonantly, making his chair emit a stern creak.

"You gentlemen are of course aware of the reasons for the amusing mystification that is required by the tradition of our craft. After all, how would it be if I had announced myself right at the start and offered my friendship to Cincinnatus C.? This, gentlemen, would have certainly resulted in repelling him, frightening him, antagonizing him—in short, I would have committed a fatal blunder."

The speaker took a sip from his glass and carefully set it aside.

He went on, batting his eyelashes: "I need not explain how precious to the success of our common undertaking is that atmosphere of warm camaraderie which, with the help of patience and kindness, is gradually created between the sentenced and the executor of the sentence. It is difficult or even impossible to recall without a shudder the barbarity of long-bygone days, when these two, not knowing each other at all, strangers to each other, but bound together by implacable law, met face to face only at the last instant before the sacrament itself. This has all been changed just as the ancient, barbaric wedding ceremony, more closely resembling a human sacrifice—when the submissive virgin was hurled by her parents into the tent of a stranger—has changed with the passing of time."

(Cincinnatus found in his pocket a piece of tinfoil chocolate wrapper and began kneading it.)

"And so, gentlemen, in order to establish the friendliest possible relations with the condemned, I moved into a gloomy cell like his, in the guise of a prisoner like him, if not more so. My innocent deception could not but succeed and therefore it would be strange for me to feel any remorse; but I do not want the cup of our friendship to be poisoned by the slightest drop of bitterness. In spite of the fact that there are witnesses present, and that I know myself to be absolutely in the right, I ask" (he stretched his hand out to Cincinnatus) "your forgiveness."

"Yes, that's real tact for you," said the director in a low voice, and his inflamed froglike eyes grew damp; he produced a folded handkerchief and was about to dab at his palpitating eyelid, but thought better of it, and instead fixed a severe, expectant gaze on Cincinnatus. The lawyer also glanced, but only in passing, as he silently moved his lips, which had begun to look like his handwriting, that is, without breaking his connection with the line, which had separated from the paper but was ready to resume its course upon it instantly.

"Your hand!" roared the director, and took such a whack at the table that he hurt his thumb.

"No, don't force him if he does not want to," M'sieur Pierre said gently. "After all, it is only a formality. Let us continue."

"Oh, righteous one," trilled Rodrig Ivanovich, bestowing upon M'sieur Pierre a glance as moist as a kiss.

"Let us continue," said M'sieur Pierre. "During this time I have succeeded in establishing a close friendship with my neighbor. We passed . . ."

Cincinnatus looked under the table. M'sieur Pierre for some reason lost countenance, began to fidget and cast a sidelong glance down. The director, lifting a corner of the oilcloth, also looked down and then glanced suspiciously at Cincinnatus. The lawyer, in his turn, made a dive, then looked around at everybody and resumed writing. Cincinnatus straightened up. (Nothing special—he had dropped his little ball of tinfoil.)

"We passed," M'sieur Pierre went on in a hurt voice, "long evenings together in constant talks, games and various amusements. Like children, we engaged in contests of strength; I, poor, weak little M'sieur Pierre naturally, oh, naturally was no match for my mighty coeval. We discussed everything—such as sex and other lofty subjects, and the hours flew by like minutes, the minutes like hours. Sometimes, in peaceful silence . . ."

Here Rodrig Ivanovich suddenly tittered. "*Impayable*, *ce* 'naturally,' " he whispered, getting the joke a little late.

". . . Sometimes, in peaceful silence, we would sit side by side, almost with our arms about each other, each thinking his own twilight thoughts, and the thoughts of both of us would flow together like rivers when we opened our lips to speak. I shared with him my experience in romance, taught him the art of chess, entertained him with a timely anecdote. And so the days passed. The results are before you. We grew to love each other, and the structure of Cincinnatus's soul is as well known to me as the structure of his neck. Thus it will be not an unfamiliar, terrible somebody but a tender friend that will help him mount the crimson steps, and he will surrender himself to me without fear—forever, for all death. Let the will of the public be carried out!" (He got up; the director got up also; the lawyer, engrossed in his writing, only rose slightly.)

"So. Now, Rodrig Ivanovich, I shall ask you to announce my title officially and to introduce me."

The director hastily put on his glasses, examined a slip of paper, and in a megaphone voice addressed Cincinnatus: "All right—This is M'sieur Pierre. *Bref*—the performer of the execution. . . . I am grateful for the honor," he added and, with an astonished expression on his face, dropped back into his chair.

"Well, you didn't manage that too well," said M'sieur Pierre with displeasure. "After all, there are certain official forms of procedure and they ought to be followed. I am certainly no pedant, but at such an important moment . . . It's no use holding your hand to your chest, you botched it, friend. No, no, stay seated, enough. Now let us continue. Roman Vissarionovich, where is the program?"

"I gave it to you," the lawyer said glibly. "However . . ." and he began to rummage in his briefcase.

"I found it, don't bother," said M'sieur Pierre, "so . . . the performance is scheduled for the day after tomorrow . . . In Thriller Square. Couldn't they have picked a better place . . . Remarkable!" (Goes on reading, muttering to himself) "Adults will be admitted . . . Circus subscription stubs will be honored . . . So, so, so . . . The performer of the execution, in red pantaloons . . . now this is nonsense— they've overdone it, as usual . . ." (To Cincinnatus) "Day after tomorrow, then. Did you understand—? And tomorrow, as our glorious custom demands, you and I must go visit the city fathers—I think you have the little list, don't you, Rodrig Ivanovich?"

Rodrig Ivanovich began to slap at various parts of his

cotton-padded body, rolling his eyes and for some reason getting up. At last the list was found.

"All righty," said M'sieur Pierre. "Add it to your file, Roman Vissarionovich. I think that does it. Now, according to the law, the floor belongs to—"

"Oh, no, *c'est vraiment superflu* ..." Rodrig Ivanovich interrupted hastily. "After all, that's a very antiquated law."

"According to the law," M'sieur Pierre repeated firmly, turning to Cincinnatus, "the floor is yours."

"Honest one!" said the director in a breaking voice, his jelly jowls shaking.

Silence ensued. The lawyer was writing so quickly that the flashing of his pencil hurt the eyes.

"I shall wait one whole minute," said M'sieur Pierre, placing a thick watch on the table before him.

The lawyer inhaled jerkily and began gathering up the thickly covered sheets.

The minute passed.

"The conference is concluded," said M'sieur Pierre. "Let us go, gentlemen. Roman Vissarionovich, you will let me look over the minutes before you have them mimeographed, won't you? No, a little later—right now my eyes are tired."

"I must admit," said the director, "in spite of myself I sometimes regret that we no longer use the sys ..." He bent over to M'sieur Pierre's ear in the doorway.

"What's that you're saying, Rodrig Ivanovich?" the lawyer inquired jealously. The director whispered it to him also.

"Yes, you're right," agreed the lawyer. "However, the

dear little law can be circumvented. For example, if we stretch the chop-chop out to several times . . ."

"Now, now," said M'sieur Pierre, "enough of that, you jokers, I never make notches."

"No, we were just speaking theoretically," the director smiled ingratiatingly; "only in the old days, when it was legal to use—" The door slammed shut, and the voices faded in the distance.

Almost immediately, however, another guest called on Cincinnatus—the librarian, coming to fetch the books. His long, pale face with its halo of dusty-black hair around a bald spot, his long tremulous torso in the bluish sweater, his long legs in the truncated trousers—all of this together created an odd, morbid impression, as if the man had been squashed and flattened out. However, it seemed to Cincinnatus that, with the book dust, a film of something remotely human had settled on the librarian.

"You must have heard," said Cincinnatus, "the day after tomorrow will be my extermination. I shan't be taking any more books."

"You will not," said the librarian.

Cincinnatus went on: "I should like to weed out a few noxious truths. Do you have a minute? I want to say that now, when I know exactly . . . How delightful was that very ignorance that so depressed me . . . No more books . . ."

"Would you like something about gods?" the librarian suggested.

"No, don't bother. I don't feel like reading that."

"Some do," said the librarian.

"Yes, I know, but really, it's not worthwhile."

"For the last night," the librarian finished his thought with difficulty.

"You are awfully talkative today," said Cincinnatus with a smile. "No, take all this away. I wasn't able to finish *Quercus!* Oh yes, by the way, this was brought me by mistake . . . these little volumes . . . Arabic, aren't they? . . . unfortunately I hadn't time to study the Oriental languages."

"Pity," said the librarian.

"It's all right, my soul will make up for it. Wait a minute, do not go yet. Although I know, of course, that you are only bound in human skin, as it were, yet . . . I am content with little . . . The day after tomorrow—"

But, trembling, the librarian left.

Seventeen

Tradition required that on the eve of the execution its passive and active participants together make a brief farewell visit to each of the chief officials; however, in order to shorten the ritual, it was decided that those persons would assemble at the suburban house of the deputy city manager (the manager himself, who was the deputy's nephew, was away, visiting friends in Pritomsk) and that Cincinnatus and M'sieur Pierre would drop in for an informal supper.

It was a dark night, and a strong warm wind was blowing when, dressed in identical capes, on foot, escorted by six soldiers carrying halberds and lanterns, they crossed the bridge and entered the sleeping city where, avoiding the main streets, they began to climb a flinty path between rustling gardens.

(Just before that, on the bridge Cincinnatus had turned, freeing his head from the hood of his cloak: the blue, elaborate, many-towered, huge bulk of the fortress rose into the dull sky, where a cloud had barred an apricot moon. The dark air above the bridge blinked and twitched because of the bats. "You promised . . . ," whispered M'sieur Pierre, giving him a slight squeeze on the elbow, and Cincinnatus again pulled on his cowl.)

This nocturnal promenade which had promised to be so rich with sad, carefree, singing, murmuring impressions— for what is a recollection, if not the soul of an impression? —proved in reality to be vague and insignificant and flashed by so quickly as happens only amid very familiar surroundings, in the dark, when the varicolored fractions of day are replaced by the integers of night.

At the end of a narrow and gloomy lane, where the gravel crunched and there was a smell of juniper, there suddenly appeared a theatrically lighted carriage porch with whitewashed columns, friezes on the pediment, and potted laurels, and hardly pausing in the vestibule, where servants flitted to and fro like birds of paradise, shedding plumes on the black and white tiles, Cincinnatus and M'sieur Pierre entered a hall buzzing with a large gathering. All were assembled here.

Here the custodian of the city fountains could be at once recognized by his characteristic shock of hair; here the telegraph chief's uniform flashed with golden medals; here, with his obscene nose, was the ruddy director of supplies; and the lion-tamer with an Italian name; and the judge, deaf and venerable; and, in green patent-leather shoes, the park administrator; and a multitude of other stately, respectable, gray-haired individuals with repulsive faces. There were no ladies present, unless one counted the district superintendent of schools, a very stout, elderly woman in a gray frock coat cut like a man's, with large flat cheeks and a smooth hairdo as shiny as steel.

Someone slipped on the parquetry, to the accompaniment of general laughter. A chandelier dropped one of its candles. Someone had already placed a bouquet on a small coffin that had been set out for exhibition. Standing apart with Cincinnatus, M'sieur Pierre was calling his charge's attention to these phenomena.

Just then, however, the host, a swarthy old man with a goatee, clapped his hands. The doors were flung open, and everyone moved into the dining room. M'sieur Pierre and Cincinnatus were seated side by side at the head of a dazzling table, and everyone began to glance, with restraint at first, then with benevolent curiosity—which in some began to turn into surreptitious tenderness—at the pair, identically clad in Elsinore jackets; then, as a lambent smile gradually appeared on M'sieur Pierre's lips and he began to talk, the eyes of the guests turned more and more openly toward him and Cincinnatus, who was unhurriedly, diligently and intently—as if seeking the solution to a problem—balancing his fish knife in various ways, now on the salt shaker, now on the incurvation of the fork, now leaning it against the slender crystal vase with a white rose that distinctly adorned his place.

The footmen, recruited from among the town's most adroit dandies—the best representatives of its purple youth

—briskly served the food (sometimes even leaping across the table with a dish), and everyone noticed the polite solicitude with which M'sieur Pierre took care of Cincinnatus, immediately switching from a conversational smile to momentary seriousness, while he carefully placed a choice morsel on Cincinnatus's plate; whereupon, with the former playful twinkle on his pink, hairless face, he would resume his witty conversation, directed to the whole table—and suddenly, leaning over just a little, grabbing the gravy boat or the pepper shaker, he would glance interrogatively at Cincinnatus; the latter, however, did not touch any of the food, but continued, just as silently, attentively and diligently, to shift the knife about.

"Your remark," M'sieur Pierre said gaily, turning to the city traffic chief, who had managed to get a word in and was now pleasurably anticipating a scintillating reply, "your remark reminds me of the well-known anecdote about the Hippocratic oath."

"Tell it, we don't know it, do tell it," voices begged him from all sides.

"I comply with your wish," said M'sieur Pierre. "To a gynecologist comes this—"

"Scuse the intermission," said the lion-tamer (gray-haired and mustachioed, with a crimson ribbon across his chest), "but is the gent convicted that the anecdotus is wholesomely for the ears of . . . ?" He emphatically indicated Cincinnatus with his eyes.

"Quite, quite," M'sieur Pierre replied sternly, "I would never allow myself the slightest impropriety in the presence of . . . As I was saying, to a gynecologist comes this little old lady" (M'sieur Pierre stuck out his lower lip slightly). "She says, 'I've got quite a serious illness and I'm afraid it'll be the death of me.' 'What are the symptoms?' asks the doctor. 'Oh doctor, my head shakes...'" and M'sieur Pierre, mumbling and shaking, mimicked the old woman.

The guests roared. At the other end of the table the deaf judge, his face in agonized contortions as if constipated with laughter, was thrusting his large, humid ear in the face of his guffawing, selfish neighbor, and, tugging at his sleeve, implored him to repeat the story of M'sieur Pierre, who, meanwhile, was jealously following the fate of his anecdote across the whole length of the table, and was satisfied only when somebody had assuaged the sufferer's curiosity.

"Your remarkable aphorism that life is a medical secret," said the custodian of fountains, creating such a spray of fine saliva that a rainbow formed near his mouth, "might very well be applied to the odd thing that happened the other day in my secretary's family. Can you imagine..."

"Well, my little Cincinnatus, are you afraid?" one of the glittering footmen asked Cincinnatus as he poured him wine; Cincinnatus looked up, it was his waggish brother-in-law. "Afraid, aren't you? Here, have a drink on the brink."

"What's going on here?" M'sieur Pierre coldly said, putting the babbler in his place, and the latter promptly stepped away, and now he was bending over with his bottle at the elbow of the next guest.

"Gentlemen!" exclaimed the host, rising from his chair and holding his glass containing an icy pale-yellow drink at the level of his starched chest. "I propose a toast to..."

"Bitter, bitter, sweeten it with a kiss," said a recent best man, and the rest of the guests joined in the chanting.

"Let us . . . a *bruderschaft* . . . I implore you—" M'sieur Pierre said to Cincinnatus in a changed voice, his face twisted in supplication, "do not refuse me this, I implore you, this is the way it is done always, always . . ."

Cincinnatus was fiddling with the curled petal tips of the moist white rose, which he had absently pulled out of the overturned vase.

". . . I have the right, finally, to demand," M'sieur Pierre whispered convulsively, and suddenly, with a gasp of forced laugh, he poured a drop of wine from his glass on top of Cincinnatus's head, and then sprinkled himself also.

Cries of "Bravo!" were heard from all sides, and neighbor would turn to neighbor, expressing in dramatic pantomime his wonder and delight, and the unbreakable glasses clinked, and heaps of apples each as big as a child's head shone among the dusty-blue bunches of grapes on a silver ship breasting the air, and the table seemed to slope up like a diamond mountain, and the many-armed chandelier journeyed through the mists of plafond art, shedding tears, shedding beams, in vain search of a landing.

"I am touched, touched," M'sieur Pierre was saying, as they took turns coming up to him to congratulate him. As they did so, some of them stumbled, and a few sang. The father of the city firemen was disgracefully drunk; two of the servants were trying stealthily to haul him away, but he sacrificed his coattails like a lizard does its tail, and remained. The respectable woman, who supervised the schools, flushing blotchily, was silently and tensely leaning away as she defended herself from the supply director, who was playfully aiming at her with his finger, which resembled a carrot, as though he were about to transfix her or tickle her, all the while repeating, "tee-tee-tee!"

"Friends, let us go out on the terrace," announced the host, whereupon Marthe's brother and the son of the late Dr. Sineokov pulled open a drapery with a rattle of wooden rings; the swaying light of painted lanterns revealed a stone veranda, bordered further by the tenpinlike uprights of a balustrade, between which showed black the hourglasses of night.

The sated guests, their bellies gurgling, settled themselves in low armchairs. Some lounged by the columns, others near the balustrade. Near it, too, stood Cincinnatus, twirling in his fingers the mummy of a cigar, and beside him, not turning to him but incessantly touching him either with his back, or with his side, M'sieur Pierre was saying to the accompaniment of approving exclamations from his listeners:

"Photography and fishing—those are my two chief passions. It may seem odd to you, but fame and honor are nothing to me compared with rural quiet. I see you are smiling skeptically, kind sir" (he said in passing to one of the guests who at once repudiated his smile), "but I swear to you that this is so, and I do not swear idly. The love of nature was bequeathed to me by my father, who never lied either. Many of you, of course, remember him and can confirm this, even in writing, if it should become necessary."

Standing by the balustrade, Cincinnatus peered vaguely into the darkness, and just then, as if by request, the darkness paled enticingly, as the moon, now clear and high, glided out from behind the black fleece of cloudlets, varnished the shrubs, and let its light trill in the ponds. Suddenly, with an abrupt start of the soul, Cincinnatus realized that he was in the very thick of the Tamara Gardens which he remembered so well and which had seemed so inaccessible to him; he realized that he had walked here with Marthe many times, past this very house in which he was now and which had then appeared to him as a white villa with boarded-up windows, glimpsed through the foliage on the hillock ... Now, exploring the surroundings with a diligent eye, he easily removed the murky film of night from the familiar lawns and also erased from them the superfluous lunar dusting, so as to make them exactly as they were in his memory. As he restored the painting smudged by the soot of night, he saw groves, paths, brooks taking shape where they used to be ... In the distance, pressing against the metallic sky, the charmed hills stood still, glossed with blue and folded in gloom. . . .

"A porch, moon's torch, and he, and she," recited M'sieur Pierre smiling at Cincinnatus, who noticed that everyone was looking at him with tender, expectant sympathy.

"Admiring the landscape?" said the park superintendent to him with a confidential air, hands clasped behind his back. "You . . ." He stopped short and, as if somewhat embarrassed, turned to M'sieur Pierre: "Excuse me . . . do I have your permission? After all I haven't been introduced . . ."

"Please, please, you don't have to ask my permission," M'sieur Pierre replied courteously and, touching Cincinnatus's elbow said in a low voice, "This gentleman would like to chat with you, my dear."

The park superintendent cleared his throat into his fist

and repeated, "The landscape ... Admiring the landscape? Right now you can't see very much. But just you wait, exactly at midnight—so our chief engineer has promised me ... Nikita Lukich! Over here, Nikita Lukich!"

"Coming," Nikita Lukich responded in a jaunty bass, and obligingly stepped forward, cheerfully turning now to one, now to the other, his youthful, fleshy face with the white brush of a mustache, and placing a hand comfortably on the shoulder of the park superintendent and on that of M'sieur Pierre.

"I was just telling him, Nikita Lukich, that you promised, exactly at midnight, in honor of ..."

"Why of course," the chief engineer interrupted. "We shall have the surprise without fail. Don't you worry about that. By the way, what time is it, boys?"

He relieved the others' shoulders of the pressure of his broad hands and, with a preoccupied mien, went inside.

"Well, in eight hours or so we shall already be in the square," said M'sieur Pierre, squeezing shut the lid of his watch. "We shan't be getting much sleep. You aren't cold, are you, my dear? The nice man said there would be a surprise. I must say they are spoiling us. That fish we had for dinner was without equal."

"... Stop it, leave me alone," said the husky voice of the lady administrator, whose massive back and gray bun were coming straight at M'sieur Pierre as she retreated from the supply director's index finger. "Tee-tee," he squeaked playfully, "tee-tee."

"Take it easy, madam," croaked M'sieur Pierre. "My corns aren't state property."

"Bewitching woman," the supply director remarked in

passing, totally without expression and, capering, headed toward a group of men standing by the columns; then his shadow was lost among their shadows, and a breeze made the Japanese lanterns sway, and in the dark there would be revealed now a hand pompously preening a mustache, now a cup raised to senile, fish lips that were trying to get the sugar from the bottom.

"Attention!" the host shouted, passing like a whirlwind among the guests.

And, first in the garden, then beyond it, then still further, along the walks, in groves, in glades and on lawns, singly and in clusters, ruby, sapphire, and topaz lamps lit up, gradually inlaying the night with gems. The guests began to "oh!" and "ah!" M'sieur Pierre inhaled sharply and grabbed Cincinnatus by the wrist. The lights covered an ever-increasing area: now they stretched out along a distant valley, now they were on the other side of it, in the form of an elongated brooch, now they already studded the first slopes; once there they passed on from hill to hill, nestling in the most secret folds, groping their way to the summits, crossing over them! "Oh, how beautiful," whispered M'sieur Pierre, for an instant pressing his cheek against the cheek of Cincinnatus.

The guests applauded. For three minutes a good million light bulbs of diverse colors burned, artfully planted in the grass, in branches, on cliffs, and all arranged in such a way as to embrace the whole nocturnal landscape with a grandiose monogram of "P" and "C," which, however, had not quite come off. Thereupon the lights went out all at once and solid darkness reached up to the terrace.

When engineer Nikita Lukich reappeared they surrounded him and wanted to toss him. It was time, how-ever, to begin thinking about a well deserved rest. Before the guests left, the host offered to photograph M'sieur Pierre and Cincinnatus by the balustrade. M'sieur Pierre, even though he was the one who was being photographed, nevertheless directed this operation. A burst of light illu-mined the white profile of Cincinnatus and the eyeless face beside him. The host himself handed them their capes and went out to see them off. In the vestibule morose soldiers were clattering sleepily as they sorted out their halberds.

"I am ineffably flattered by your visit," the host said to Cincinnatus in parting. "Tomorrow—or rather this morn-ing—I shall be there, of course, and not only in an official capacity but also in a personal one. My nephew tells me that a large gathering is expected.

"Well, good luck to you," said he to M'sieur Pierre in between the traditional three kisses on the cheeks.

Cincinnatus and M'sieur Pierre, with their escort of sol-diers, plunged into the lane.

"On the whole you are a good fellow," said M'sieur Pierre when they had gone a little distance, "only why do you always. . . . Your shyness makes an extremely unfavorable impression on new people. I don't know about you," he added, "but although I am delighted with the illumination and so forth, I have heartburn and a suspicion that not all the cooking was done with creamery butter."

They walked a long time. It was very dark and foggy.

A blunt knock-knock-knock came from somewhere off to the left as they were descending Steep Avenue. Knock-knock-knock.

"The scoundrels," muttered M'sieur Pierre. "Didn't they swear it was all done?"

At last they crossed the bridge and started uphill. The moon had already been removed and the dark towers of the fortress blended with the clouds.

At the third gate, Rodrig Ivanovich was waiting in dressing gown and nightcap.

"Well, how was it?" he asked impatiently.

"Nobody missed you," M'sieur Pierre said dryly.

Eighteen

"Tried to sleep, could not, only got chilled all through, and now it is dawn" (Cincinnatus wrote rapidly, illegibly, leaving words unfinished, as a running man leaves an incomplete footprint), "now the air is pale, and I am so frozen that it seems to me that the abstract concept of 'cold' must have as its concrete form the shape of my body, and they are going to come for me any time now. It makes me ashamed to be afraid, but I am desperately afraid—fear, never halting, rushes through me with an ominous roar, like a torrent, and my body vibrates like a bridge over a waterfall, and one has to speak very loud to hear oneself above the roar. I am ashamed, my soul has disgraced itself—for this ought not to be, *ne dolzhno bïlo*

bï bïť—only on the bark of the Russian language could such a fungus bunch of verbs have sprouted—oh, how ashamed I am that my attention is occupied, my soul blocked by such dithering details, they push through, with lips wet, to say farewell, all kinds of memories come to say farewell: I, a child, am sitting with a book in the hot sun on the bank of a dinning stream, and the water throws its wavering reflection on the lines of an old, old poem,—'Love at the sloping of our years'—but I know I should not yield—'Becomes more tender and superstitious'—neither to memories, nor to fear, nor to this passionate syncope: '... and superstitious'—and I had hoped so much that everything would be orderly, all simple and neat. For I know that the horror of death is nothing really, a harmless convulsion—perhaps even healthful for the soul—the choking wail of a newborn child or a furious refusal to release a toy—and that there once lived, in caverns where there is the tinkle of a perpetual stillicide, and stalactites, sages who rejoiced at death and who—blunderers for the most part, it is true—yet who in their own way, mastered—and even though I know all this, and know yet another main, paramount thing that no one here knows—nevertheless, look, dummies, how afraid I am, how everything in me trembles, and dins, and rushes—and any moment now they will come for me, and I am not ready, I am ashamed ..."

Cincinnatus got up, made a running start and smashed headlong into the wall—the real Cincinnatus, however, remained sitting at the table, staring at the wall, chewing his pencil, and presently shuffled his feet under the table and continued to write, a little less rapidly:

"Save these jottings—I do not know whom I ask, but save these jottings—I assure you that such a law exists, look it up, you will see!—let them lie around for a while— how can that hurt you?—and I ask you so earnestly—my last wish—how can you not grant it? I must have at least the theoretical possibility of having a reader, otherwise, really, I might as well tear it all up. There, that is what I needed to say. Now it is time to get ready."

He paused again. It had already grown quite light in the cell, and Cincinnatus knew by the position of the light that half-past five was about to strike. He waited until he heard the distant ringing, and went on writing, but now quite slowly and haltingly, just as if he had spent all his strength on some initial exclamation.

"My words all mill about in one spot," wrote Cincinnatus. "Envious of poets. How wonderful it must be to speed along a page and, right from the page, where only a shadow continues to run, to take off into the blue. The untidiness, sloppiness of an execution, of all the manipulations, before and after. How cold the blade, how smooth the ax's grip. With emery paper. I suppose the pain of parting will be red and loud. The thought, when written down, becomes less oppressive, but some thoughts are like a cancerous tumor: you express it, you excise it, and it grows back worse than before. It is hard to imagine that this very morning, in an hour or two . . ."

But two hours passed, and more, and, just as always, Rodion brought breakfast, tidied the cell, sharpened the pencil, removed the close-stool, fed the spider. Cincinnatus did not ask him anything, but, when Rodion had left, and time dragged on at its customary trot, he realized that once again he had been duped, that he had strained his soul to no purpose, and that everything had remained just as uncertain, viscous and senseless as before.

The clock had just finished striking three or four (he had dozed off and then half awakened, and so had not counted the strokes, but had only retained an approximate impression of their sum of sound) when suddenly the door opened and Marthe came in. Her cheeks were flushed, the comb at the back of her head had worked loose, the tight bodice of her black velvet dress was heaving—and something did not fit right, and this made her appear lopsided, and she kept trying to straighten her dress, tugging at it, or very rapidly wriggling her hips, as if something underneath were wrong and uncomfortable.

"Some cornflowers for you," she said, tossing a blue posy upon the table, and at the same time, nimbly lifting the hem of her skirt above her knee, she put on the chair a plump little leg in a white stocking, pulling it up to the place where the garter had left its imprint on the tender, quivering fat. "My, how hard it was to get permission! Of course, I had to agree to a little concession—the usual story. Well, how are you, my poor little Cin-Cin?"

"I must confess I was not expecting you," said Cincinnatus. "Sit down somewhere."

"I tried yesterday, no luck—and today I said to myself, I'll get through if it's the last thing I do. He kept me for an hour, your director. Spoke *very* highly of you, by the way. Oh, how I hurried today, how I was afraid that I would be too late. What a mob there was in Thriller Square this morning!"

"Why did they call it off?" asked Cincinnatus.

"Well, they said everybody was tired, didn't get enough sleep. You know, the crowd simply did not want to leave. You ought to be proud."

Oblong, marvelously burnished tears crept down Marthe's cheeks and chin, closely following all their contours—one even flowed down her neck as far as the clavicular dimple ... Her eyes, however, kept on gazing just as roundly, her short fingers with white spots on the nails kept spreading out, and her thin mobile lips kept emitting words:

"There are some who insist that now it's been postponed for a long time, but then you can't really find out from anyone. You simply cannot imagine all the rumors, the confusion ..."

"What are you crying about?" asked Cincinnatus with a smile.

"I don't know myself—I'm just worn out ..." (In a low chesty voice): "I'm sick and tired of all of you. Cincinnatus, Cincinnatus, what a mess you have got yourself into! ... The things people say about you—it's dreadful! Oh, listen," she suddenly began in a different tempo, beaming, smacking her lips, and preening herself. "The other day—when was it?—yes, day before yesterday, there comes to me this little dame, a lady doctor or something—a total stranger, mind you, in an awful raincoat, and begins hawing and hemming. 'Of course,' she says, 'you understand.' I says, 'No, so far I don't understand a thing.' She says:— 'Oh, I know who you are, you don't know me' ... I says ..." (Marthe miming her interlocutress, assumed a fussy and fatuous tone, slowing soberly, however, on the drawn-out "says," and, now that she was conveying her own words, she depicted herself as being calm as snow). "In a word,

she tried to tell me that she was your mother—though I
think even her age wouldn't be right, but we'll overlook that.
She said she was terribly afraid of being persecuted, since,
you see, they had questioned her and subjected her to all
sorts of things. I says: 'What do I have to do with all this
and why should you want to see me?' She says: 'Oh, yes, I
know you are terribly kind, you'll do all you can.' I says:
'What makes you think I'm kind?' She says: 'Oh, I know'—
and asks if I couldn't give her a paper, a certificate, that I
would sign hand and foot, stating that she had never been
at our house and had never seen you ... This, you know,
seemed so funny to Marthe, so funny! I think" (in a drawl-
ing, low-pitched voice) "that she must have been some
kind of a crank, a nut, don't you think so? In any case, I
of course did not give her anything. Victor and the others
said it might compromise me—since it would seem that
I knew your every move, if I knew you weren't acquainted
with her—and so she left, very crestfallen, I would say."

"But it really *was* my mother," said Cincinnatus.

"Maybe, maybe. After all, it's not so important. But tell
me, why are you so dull and glum, Cin-Cin? I imagined
you would be so happy to see me, but you ..."

She glanced at the cot, then at the door.

"I don't know what the rules are here," she said under
her breath, "but if you need it badly, Cin-Cin, go ahead,
only do it quickly."

"Oh, don't—what nonsense," said Cincinnatus.

"Well, as you please. I only wanted to give you a treat
because it's the last interview and all that. Oh, by the way,
do you know who wants to marry me? Guess who—you'll
never guess. Remember that old grouch who used to live

next door to us, who kept stinking with his pipe across the fence, and always used to peek when I climbed the apple tree? Can you imagine? And the thing is, he was perfectly serious! Can you see me marrying him, the old scarecrow? Ugh! Anyway I feel it's time I had a good, long rest—you know, close my eyes, stretch out, not think about anything, and relax, absolutely alone of course or else with someone who would really care, and understand everything, everything . . .''

Her short, coarse eyelashes again glistened, and the tears crept down, visiting every dimple on her apple-rosy cheeks.

Cincinnatus took one of these tears and tasted it: it was neither salty nor sweet—merely a drop of luke-warm water. Cincinnatus did not do this.

Suddenly the door squealed and opened an inch; a red-haired finger beckoned to Marthe. She quickly went to the door.

"Well, what do you want, it isn't time yet, is it, I was promised a whole hour," she whispered rapidly. Something was said in reply.

"Not on your life!" she said indignantly. "You can tell him that. The agreement was that I should do it only with the direct—"

She was interrupted; she listened carefully to the insistent mumbling; she looked down, frowning, and scraping the floor with the toe of her slipper.

"Well, all right," she blurted out, and with innocent vivacity turned to her husband: "I'll be back in five minutes, Cin-Cin."

(While she was gone he thought that not only had he not even begun his urgent talk with her, but that now he could no longer formulate those important things ... At the same time his heart was aching, and the same old memory whimpered in a corner; but it was time, it was time to wean himself from all this anguish.)

She returned only in three quarters of an hour, snorting contemptuously. She put one foot on the chair, snapped her garter, and, angrily readjusting the pleats below her waist, sat down at the table, precisely as she had been sitting before.

"All for nothing," she said with a sneer and began fingering the blue flowers on the table. "Well, why don't you tell me something, my little Cin-Cin, my cockerel? ... You know I picked them myself, I don't care for poppies, but these are lovely. Shouldn't try if you can't manage it," she added unexpectedly in a different tone of voice, narrowing her eyes. "No, Cin-Cin, I wasn't speaking to you." (Sigh) "Well, tell me something, console me."

"My letter—did you ..." began Cincinnatus, then cleared his throat. "Did you read my letter carefully?"

"Please, please," cried Marthe, clutching her temples, "let's talk about anything but that letter!"

"No, let us talk about it," said Cincinnatus.

She jumped up, spasmodically straightening her dress, and began speaking incoherently, lisping a little, as she did when she was angry. "That was a horrible letter, that was some kind of delirium, I didn't understand it, anyway; one might have thought you had been sitting here alone with a bottle and writing. I didn't want to bring up that letter, but now that you ... Listen, you know the transmitters read it—they copied it, and they said to themselves, 'Oho! She must be in cahoots with him, if he writes to her like that.' Can't you see, I don't want to know anything about your affairs, you have no right to send me such letters, to drag me into your criminal—"

"I did not write you anything criminal," said Cincinnatus.

"That's what you think, but everyone was horrified by your letter, simply horrified! Me, I'm stupid maybe, and don't know anything about the laws, but still my instinct told me that every word of yours was impossible, unspeakable . . . Oh, Cincinnatus, what a position you put me in— and the children—think of the children. . . . Listen—please listen to me for just a minute—" she went on with such ardor that her speech became quite unintelligible, "renounce everything, everything. Tell them that you are innocent, that you were merely swaggering, tell them, repent, do it—even if it doesn't save your head, think of me—already they are pointing fingers at me and saying, 'That's her, the widow, that's her!' "

"Wait, Marthe, I don't understand. Repent of what?"

"That's right! Mix me up in it, ask me leading . . . If I knew all the answers, why, then I'd be your accomac . . . accomplice! That's quite obvious. No, enough, enough. I'm dreadfully afraid of all this . . . Tell me one last time, are you sure you don't want to repent, for my sake, for all our sakes?"

"Good-bye, Marthe," said Cincinnatus.

She sat down and lapsed into thought, leaning on her right elbow, and sketching her world on the table with her left hand.

"How dreadful, how dull," she said, heaving a deep, deep sigh. She frowned and drew a river with her fingernail. "I thought we would meet quite differently. I was ready to

give you everything. And this is what I get for my pains!
Well, what's done is done." (The river flowed into a sea—
off. the edge of the table.) "You know, I'm leaving with a
heavy heart. Yes, but how am I going to get out?" she remembered suddenly, innocently and even cheerfully. "They
won't be coming for me for a while yet, I talked them into
giving me oodles of time."

"Don't worry," said Cincinnatus, "every word we say . . .
They will open it in a moment."

He was not mistaken.

"Bye, bye-bye," chirped Marthe. "Wait, stop pawing me,
let me say good-bye to my husband. Bye-bye. If you need
anything in the way of shirts or anything . . . Oh yes, the
children asked me to give you a big, big kiss. There was
something else . . . Oh, I nearly forgot—daddy took the
wine-cup I gave you—he says you promised him—"

"Hurry, hurry, little lady," interrupted Rodion, kneeing
her in familiar fashion toward the door.

Nineteen

Next morning they brought him the news-
papers, and this reminded him of the first days of his confinement. He noticed at once the color photograph: under
a blue sky, the square, packed so densely with a motley
crowd that only the very edge of the red platform was
visible. In the column dealing with the execution half the
lines were blacked out, and out of the remainder Cincinnatus could fish only what he already knew from Marthe—
that the maestro was not feeling too well, and that the performance was postponed, possibly for a long time.

"What a treat you are getting today," said Rodion, not
to Cincinnatus but to the spider.

In both hands, most carefully, but at the same time

squeamishly (care prompted him to press it to his chest, distaste made him hold it away) he carried a towel gathered together in a lump in which something large stirred and rustled.

"Got it on a window pane in the tower. The monster! See how it flops and flaps—you can hardly hold it . . ."

He was going to pull up the chair, as he always did, in order to stand up on it and deliver the victim to the voracious spider on his solid web (the beast was already puffing himself up, sensing the prey) but something went wrong—his gnarled, fearful fingers happened to release the main fold of the towel, and he immediately cried out and cringed, as people cry out and cringe whom not a bat but an ordinary house mouse inspires with revulsion and terror. Something large, dark, and furnished with feelers, disengaged itself from the towel, and Rodion emitted a loud yell, tramping in one place, afraid to let the thing escape but not daring to grab it. The towel fell; and the fair captive clung to Rodion's cuff, clutching it with all six of its adhesive feet.

It was only a moth, but what a moth! It was as large as a man's hand; it had thick, dark-brown wings with a hoary lining and gray-dusted margins; each wing was adorned in the center with an eye-spot, shining like steel.

Its segmented limbs, in fluffy muffs, now clung, now unstuck themselves, and the upraised vanes of its wings, through whose underside the same staring spots and wavy gray pattern showed, oscillated slowly, as the moth, groping its way, crawled up the sleeve, while Rodion, quite panic-stricken, rolling his eyes, throwing away, and forsaking his own arm, wailed, "Take it off'n me! take it off'n me!"

Upon reaching his elbow, the moth began noiselessly

flapping its heavy wings; they seemed to outbalance its body, and on Rodion's elbow joint, the creature turned over, wings hanging down, still tenaciously clinging to the sleeve—and now one could see its brown, white-dappled abdomen, its squirrel face, the black globules of its eyes and its feathery antennae resembling pointed ears.

"Take it away!" implored Rodion, beside himself, and his frantic gesturing caused the splendid insect to fall off; it struck the table, paused on it in mighty vibration, and suddenly took off from its edge.

But to me your daytime is dark, why did you disturb my slumber? Its flight, swooping and lumbering, lasted only a short time. Rodion picked up the towel and, swinging wildly, attempted to knock down the blind flyer; but suddenly it disappeared as if the very air had swallowed it.

Rodion searched for a while, did not find it, and stopped in the center of the cell, turning toward Cincinnatus, arms akimbo. "Eh? What a rascal!" he ejaculated after an expressive silence. He spat; he shook his head and pulled out a throbbing match box with spare flies, with which the disappointed animal had to be satisfied. Cincinnatus, however, had seen perfectly well where the moth had settled.

When at last Rodion departed, crossly removing his beard together with his shaggy cap of hair, Cincinnatus walked from the cot to the table. He was sorry he had returned all the books, and sat down to write to pass the time.

"Everything has fallen into place" he wrote, "that is, everything has duped me—all of this theatrical, pathetic stuff—the promises of a volatile maiden, a mother's moist gaze, the knocking on the wall, a neighbor's friendliness, and, finally, those hills which broke out in a deadly rash. Everything has duped me as it fell into place, everything. This is the dead end of this life, and I should not have sought salvation within its confines. It is strange that I should have sought salvation. Just like a man grieving because he has recently lost in his dreams some thing that he had never had in reality, or hoping that tomorrow he would dream that he found it again. That is how mathematics is created; it has its fatal flaw. I have discovered it. I have discovered the little crack in life, where it broke off, where it had once been soldered to something else, something genuinely alive, important and vast—how capacious my epithets must be in order that I may pour them full of crystalline sense . . . it is best to leave some things unsaid, or else I shall get confused again. Within this irreparable little crack decay has set in—ah, I think I shall yet be able to express it all—the dreams, the coalescence, the disintegration—no, again I am off the track—all my best words are deserters and do not answer the trumpet call, and the remainder are cripples. Oh, if only I had known that I was yet to remain here for such a long time, I would have begun at the beginning and gradually, along a high road of logically connected ideas, would have attained, would have completed, my soul would have surrounded itself with a structure of words. . . . Everything that I have written here so far is only the froth of my excitement, a senseless transport, for the very reason that I have been in such a hurry. But now, when I am hardened, when I am almost fearless of . . ."

Here the page ended, and Cincinnatus realized that he

was out of paper. However he managed to dig up one more sheet.

". . . death," he wrote on it, continuing his sentence, but he immediately crossed out that word; he must say it differently, with greater precision: "execution," perhaps, "pain" or "parting"—something like that; twirling the stunted pencil in his fingers, he paused in thought, and a little brown fuzz had stuck to the edge of the table where the moth had quivered only a short time ago, and Cincinnatus, remembering it, walked away from the table, leaving on it the blank sheet with only the one solitary word on it, and that one crossed out, and bent down (pretending that he was fixing the back of his slipper) by the cot, on whose iron leg, quite near the floor, it was settled, asleep, its visionary wings spread in solemn invulnerable torpor; only he was sorry for the downy back where the fuzz had rubbed off leaving a bald spot, as shiny as a chestnut—but the great dark wings, with their ashen edges and perpetually open eyes, were inviolable—the forewings, lowered slightly, lapped over the hind ones, and this drooping attitude might have been one of somnolent fragility, were it not for the monolithic straightness of the upper margins and the perfect symmetry of all the diverging lines—and this was so enchanting that Cincinnatus, unable to restrain himself, stroked with his fingertip the hoary ridge near the base of the right wing, then the ridge of the left one (what gentle firmness! what unyielding gentleness!); the moth, however, did not awaken, and he straightened up and, sighing slightly, moved away; he was about to sit down at the table again when suddenly the key scraped in the lock and the door opened, whining, rattling and groaning in keeping with all the rules of carceral counterpoint. Rosy M'sieur Pierre, in a pea-green hunting habit, first inserted his head and then came in completely, and behind him came two others, whom it was almost impossible to recognize as the director and the lawyer: haggard, pallid, both dressed in coarse gray shirts, shabbily shod—without any makeup, without padding and without wigs, with rheumy eyes, with scrawny bodies that one could glimpse through candid rips —they turned out to resemble each other, and their identical heads moved identically on their thin necks, pale bald bumpy heads, with a bluish stipple on the sides and protruding ears.

Attractively rouged M'sieur Pierre bowed, bringing together his patent-leather boot tops, and said in a comic falsetto:

"The carriage is waiting, if you please, sir."

"Where are we going?" asked Cincinnatus, genuinely not understanding at first, so convinced had he been that it must happen at dawn.

"Where, where . . ." M'sieur Pierre mimicked him. "You know where. Off to do chop-chop."

"But we don't have to go this very minute, do we?" asked Cincinnatus, and was himself surprised at what he was saying, "I haven't quite prepared myself . . ." (Cincinnatus is that you speaking?)

"Yes, this very minute. Good heavens, my friend, you have had nearly three weeks to prepare yourself. One would think that's sufficient. These are my assistants, Rod and Rom, please be kind to them. They may be puny-looking fellows, but they are diligent."

"We do our best," droned the fellows.

"I almost forgot," continued M'sieur Pierre. "According to the law you are still entitled to ... Roman, old boy, would you hand me the list?"

Roman, exaggeratedly hurrying, produced from under the lining of his cap a black-bordered card, folded in two; while he was getting it out, Rodrig kept mechanically tapping his sides, and seemed to be searching in his breast pockets, without taking his imbecile eyes off his comrade.

"For the sake of simplicity," said M'sieur Pierre, "here is a prepared menu of last wishes. You may choose one and only one. I shall read it aloud. Now then: a glass of wine; or a brief trip to the toilet; or a cursory inspection of the prison collection of French postcards; or ... what's this ... number four—composing an address to the director expressing ... expressing gratitude for his considerate ... Well, I never! Rodrig, you scoundrel, you have added this yourself. I don't understand, how you dared. This is an official document! Why, this is a personal insult especially when I am so meticulous in regard to the laws, when I try so hard ..."

In his anger M'sieur Pierre flung the card to the floor; Rodrig immediately picked it up, smoothed it out, muttering guiltily, "Don't you worry ... it wasn't me, Romka was the joker ... I know the regulations. Everything is in order here ... all the desires *du jour* ... or else à la carte ..."

"Outrageous! Intolerable!" M'sieur Pierre was shouting as he paced up and down the cell. "I am not well, and in spite of that I am carrying out my duties. They serve me with spoiled fish, they offer me a disgusting whore, they treat me with unheard of disrespect, and then they expect clean work from me. No sir! Enough! The cup of long-suffering has been drained! I simply refuse—do it yourselves, chop, butcher as best you can, wreck my instrument . . ."

"The public idolizes you," said obsequious Roman. "We beseech you, be calm, maestro. If something was not just right, it was the result of an oversight, a foolish mistake, an overzealous, foolish mistake, and only that! So please forgive us. Won't the pet of women, the darling of everyone, put aside that wrathful expression for the smile with which he is wont to drive to distraction. . . ."

"That'll do, that'll do, smooth talker," said M'sieur Pierre, relenting a little. "Anyway I perform my duty more conscientiously than others I could name. All right, I forgive you. But we still have to decide about that damned last wish. Well, what have you selected?" he asked Cincinnatus (who had quietly sat down on the cot). "Come on, come on. I want to get it over with, and the squeamish don't have to look."

"To finish writing something," whispered Cincinnatus half questioningly but then he frowned, straining his thoughts, and suddenly understood that everything had in fact been written already.

"I don't understand what he is saying," said M'sieur Pierre. "Perhaps someone understands, but I don't."

Cincinnatus raised his head. "Here is what I would like," he spoke clearly, "I ask three minutes—go away for that time or at least be quiet—yes, a three-minute intermission— after that, so be it, I'll act to the end my role in your idiotic production."

"Let us compromise at two and a half minutes," said M'sieur Pierre, taking out his thick watch. "Concede half a minute, won't you, friend? You won't? Well, be a robber then—I agree to it."

He leaned against the wall in a relaxed pose; Roman and Rodrig followed his example, but Rodrig's foot twisted under him and he nearly fell, casting a panic-stricken look at the maestro.

"Sh-sh, you son of a bitch," M'sieur Pierre hissed. "And anyway, why are you making yourselves so comfortable? Hands out of your pockets! Look out!" (Still rumbling he sat down on the chair.) "Rod, I have a job for you—you can gradually begin cleaning up here; just don't make too much noise."

A broom was handed Rodrig through the door and he set to work.

First of all, with the end of the broom, he knocked out the whole grating in the recess of the window; there came a distant, feeble "hurrah," as if from an abyss, and a gust of fresh air entered the cell—the sheets of paper flew off the table, and Rodrig scuffed them into a corner. Then, with the broom, he pulled down the thick gray cobweb and with it the spider, which he had once nursed with such care. To while away the time Roman picked up the spider. Crudely but cleverly made, it consisted of a round plush body with twitching legs made of springs, and, there was, attached to the middle of its back, a long elastic, by the end of which Roman was holding it suspended, moving his hand up and down so that the elastic alternately contracted and extended and the spider rose and fell. M'sieur Pierre cast a sidelong cold glance at the toy and Roman, raising his eyebrows, hastily pocketed it. Rod, meanwhile, wanted to pull out the drawer of the table, tugged with all his strength, budged it, and the table split in two. At the same time the chair on which M'sieur Pierre was seated emitted a plaintive sound, something gave, and M'sieur Pierre nearly dropped his watch. Plaster began to fall from the ceiling. A crack described a tortuous course across the wall. The cell, no longer needed, was quite obviously disintegrating.

". . . Fifty-eight, fifty-nine, sixty," counted M'sieur Pierre. "That's all. Up, please. It's a fine day, the ride will be most enjoyable, anyone else in your place would be in a hurry to start."

"Just an instant more. I find it ludicrous and disgraceful that my hands should tremble so—but I can neither stop nor hide it, and, yes, they tremble and that's all. My papers you will destroy, the rubbish you will sweep out, the moth will fly away at night through the broken window, so that nothing of me will remain within these four walls, which are already about to crumble. But now dust and oblivion are nothing to me; I feel only one thing—fear, fear, shameful, futile fear . . ." Actually Cincinnatus did not say all this; he was silently changing his shoes. The vein on his forehead was swollen, the blond locks fell on it, his shirt had a wide-open embroidered collar, which imparted a certain extraordinarily youthful quality to his neck and to his flushed face with its blond quivering mustache.

"Let's go!" shrieked M'sieur Pierre.

Cincinnatus, trying not to brush against anyone or anything, placing his feet as if he were walking on bare, sloping ice, finally made his way out of the cell, which in fact was no longer there.

Twenty

Cincinnatus was led through stone passageways. Now ahead, now behind, a distracted echo would leap out—all its burrows were crumbling. Often there were stretches of darkness because bulbs had burned out. M'sieur Pierre demanded that they go in step.

Now they were joined by several soldiers in the regulation canine masks, and then Rodrig and Roman, with the master's permission, went on ahead, with long, pleased strides, swinging their arms in businesslike fashion, and overtaking each other. Shouting, they disappeared around a corner.

Cincinnatus, who, alas, had suddenly lost the capacity of walking, was supported by M'sieur Pierre and a soldier with the face of a borzoi. For a very long time they clambered up and down staircases—the fortress must have suffered a mild stroke, as the descending stairs were in reality ascending and vice versa. Again there were long corridors, but of a more inhabited kind; that is, they visibly demonstrated— either by linoleum, or by wallpaper, or by a sea chest against the wall—that they adjoined living quarters. At one bend there was even a smell of cabbage soup. Further on they passed a glass door with the inscription "ffice," and after another period of darkness they abruptly found themselves in the courtyard, vibrant with the noonday sun.

Throughout this whole journey Cincinnatus was busy trying to cope with his choking, wrenching, implacable fear. He realized that this fear was dragging him precisely into that false logic of things that had gradually developed around him, but from which he had still somehow been able to escape that morning. The very thought that this chubby, red-cheeked hunter was going to hack at him was already an inadmissible sickening weakness, drawing Cincinnatus into a system that was perilous to him. He fully understood all this, but, like a man unable to resist arguing with a hallucination, even though he knows perfectly well that the entire masquerade is staged in his own brain, Cincinnatus tried in vain to out-wrangle his fear, despite his understanding that he ought actually to rejoice at the awakening whose proximity was presaged by barely noticeable phenomena, by the peculiar effects on everyday implements, by a certain general instability, by a certain flaw in all visible matter—but the sun was still realistic, the world still held together, objects still observed an outward propriety.

Outside the third gate the carriage was waiting. The soldiers did not accompany them further, but sat down on logs piled by the wall, and began taking off their cloth masks. The prison staff and the guards' families pressed timidly and greedily around the gate—barefoot children would run out, trying to get into the picture, and immediately would dart back, and their kerchiefed mothers would shush them, and the hot light gilded the scattered straw, and there was the odor of warm nettles, while off to one side a dozen geese crowded, gobbling discreetly.

"Well, let's get going," M'sieur Pierre said jauntily and put on his pea-green hat with a pheasant feather.

An old, scarred carriage, which listed with a groan when springy little M'sieur Pierre mounted the step, was hitched to a bay nag with bared teeth, with lesions shiny from flies on its sharply protruding haunches, all in all so lean and so ribby that its trunk seemed to be enclosed in a set of hoops. There was a red ribbon in its mane. M'sieur Pierre squeezed over to make room for Cincinnatus and asked if the bulky case that was placed at their feet were in his way. "Please, my dear fellow, try not to step on it," he added. Rodrig and Roman climbed on the box. Rodrig, who was playing the coachman, snapped the long whip, the horse gave a start, was unable to move the carriage immediately and sank on its haunches. A discordant cheer inopportunely rang out from the staff. Rising and leaning forward, Rodrig gave the horse's nose a lash, and, when the carriage moved spasmodically off, he nearly fell backwards on the box from the jolt, drawing the rein tight and crying "whoa!"

"Easy, easy," said M'sieur Pierre with a smile, touching Rodrig's back with a plump hand in a smart glove.

The pale road coiled several times, with evil picturesqueness, around the base of the fortress. In places the grade was fairly steep, and then Rodrig would hastily wind tight the scrunching brake handle. M'sieur Pierre, his hands resting on the bulldog head of his cane, gaily looked around at the cliffs, the green inclines between them, the clover and vines, and the whirling white dust, and, while he was at it, also caressed with his gaze the profile of Cincinnatus who was still engaged in his inner struggle. The scrawny, gray, bent backs of the two men sitting on the box were perfectly identical. The hoofs clipped and clopped. Horseflies circled like satellites. At times the carriage overtook hurrying pilgrims (the prison cook, for instance, with his wife), who would stop, shielding themselves from the sun and dust, and then quicken their pace. One more turn and then the road stretched out toward the bridge, having disentangled itself from the slowly revolving fortress (which already stood quite poorly, the perspective was disorganized, something had come loose and dangled).

"I'm sorry I flared up like that," M'sieur Pierre was saying gently. "Don't be angry with me, duckie. You understand yourself how it hurts to see others being sloppy when you put your whole soul into your work."

They clattered across the bridge. News of the execution had only just now begun to spread through the town. Red and blue boys ran after the carriage. A man who feigned insanity, an old fellow of Jewish origin who had for many years been fishing for nonexistent fish in a waterless river, was collecting his chattels, hurrying to join the very first group of townspeople heading for Thriller Square.

"... but there's no point in dwelling on that," M'sieur

Pierre was saying. "Men of my temperament are volatile but also get over it quickly. Rather let us turn our attention to the conduct of the fair sex."

Several girls, hatless, jostling and squealing, were buying up all the flowers from a fat flower vendor with browned breasts, and the boldest among them managed to throw a bouquet into the carriage, nearly knocking the cap off Roman's head. M'sieur Pierre shook a finger.

The horse, its bleary eye looking askance at the flat, spotted dogs, extending their bodies as they raced at its hoofs, strained up Garden Street, and the crowd was already catching up—another bouquet hit the carriage. Now they were turning right, past the huge ruins of the ancient factory, then along Telegraph Street, already ringing, moaning, tooting with the noise of instruments tuning up, then through an unpaved, whispering lane, past a public garden where two bearded men in civilian dress got up from a bench when they saw the carriage, and, gesticulating emphatically, began indicating it to each other—both dreadfully excited, square-shouldered—and now they were running, energetically and angularly lifting their legs, toward the same place as everyone else. Beyond the public garden the corpulent white statue had been split in two—by a thunderbolt, said the papers.

"In a moment we shall be driving past your house," said M'sieur Pierre very softly.

Roman began fidgeting on the box and twisting around to Cincinnatus, cried:

"In a moment we shall be driving past your house," and at once he turned away again, bouncing up and down, like a pleased urchin.

Cincinnatus did not want to look, but still he looked. Marthe was sitting in the branches of the barren apple tree waving a handkerchief, while in the garden next door, among sunflowers and hollyhocks, a scarecrow in a crushed top hat was waving its sleeve. The wall of the house, especially at the spots where leafy shadows had once played, had peeled strangely, and part of the roof—But they had driven past.

"Really, there is something heartless about you," said M'sieur Pierre with a sigh and impatiently stuck his cane into the back of the driver, who rose slightly and, with frenzied lashings of his whip, achieved a miracle: the nag broke into a gallop.

Now they were driving along the boulevard. The agitation in the city continued to mount. The motley façades of the houses swayed and flapped, as they were hastily decorated with welcoming posters. One small house was especially well decked out: its door opened quickly, a youth came out, and his entire family followed to see him off—this day he had reached execution-attending age; mother was smiling through her tears, granny was thrusting a sandwich into his knapsack, kid brother was handing him his staff. The ancient stone bridges arching above the streets (once such a boon to pedestrians, but now used only by gawkers and street supervisors) were already teeming with photographers. M'sieur Pierre kept tipping his hat. Dandies on their shiny clockwork cycles passed the carriage and craned their necks. A person in Turkish trousers came running out of a café with a pail of confetti, but, missing, sent his varicolored blizzard into the face of a cropped fellow who had just come running from the opposite sidewalk with a bien-venue platter of "bread and salt."

All that remained of the statue of Captain Somnus was the legs up to the hips, surrounded by roses—it too must have been struck by lightning. Somewhere ahead a brass band was scorching away at the march "*Golubchik*." White clouds moved jerkily across the whole sky—I think the same ones pass over and over again, I think there are only three kinds, I think it is all stage-setting, with a suspicious green tinge . . .

"Now, now, come on, no foolishness," said M'sieur Pierre. "Don't you dare start fainting. It's unworthy of a man."

And now they had arrived. There were as yet relatively few spectators, but they continued to flow in endlessly. In the center of the plaza—no, not quite in the center, that precisely was the dreadful part—rose the vermilion platform of the scaffold. The old electrically powered municipal hearse stood modestly at a slight distance. A combined brigade of telegraphers and firemen was maintaining order. The band was apparently playing with all its might, since the conductor, a one-legged cripple, was waving furiously; now, however, not a sound was audible.

M'sieur Pierre, raising his plump shoulders, climbed gracefully out of the carriage and immediately turned, wishing to assist Cincinnatus, but Cincinnatus got out from the other side. There was some booing.

Rodrig and Roman hopped off the box; all three pressed around Cincinnatus.

"By myself," said Cincinnatus.

It was about twenty paces to the scaffold, and, in order

that no one might touch him, Cincinnatus was compelled to trot. Somewhere in the crowd a dog barked. Upon reaching the crimson steps, Cincinnatus stopped. M'sieur Pierre took him by the elbow.

"By myself," said Cincinnatus.

He mounted the platform, where the block was, that is, a smooth, sloping slab of polished oak, of sufficient size so that one could easily lie on it with outspread arms. M'sieur Pierre climbed up also. The public buzzed.

While they were fussing with the buckets and spreading the sawdust, Cincinnatus, not knowing what to do, leaned against the wooden railing, but a slight tremor was running all through it and some curious spectators below started to palpate his ankles; he moved away and, a little short of breath, wetting his lips, his arms folded somewhat awkwardly across his chest, as if he did it for the first time, he began looking around. Something had happened to the lighting, there was something wrong with the sun, and a section of the sky was shaking. Poplars had been planted around the square, but they were stiff and rickety—one of them was very slowly . . .

But again a buzzing noise passed through the crowd: Rodrig and Roman, stumbling, shoving against each other, puffing and grunting, clumsily carried the heavy case up the steps and plunked it down on the board floor. M'sieur Pierre threw off his jacket remaining clad in a singlet. A turquoise woman was tattooed on his white biceps, while, in one of the first rows of the crowd, which was pressing around the very scaffold (regardless of the firemen's entreaties), stood the same woman in the flesh, and also her two sisters, as well as the little old man with the fishing rod, and the tanned flower woman, and the youth with his staff, and one of Cincinnatus's brothers-in-law, and the librarian, reading a newspaper, and that stout fellow Nikita Lukich the engineer—and Cincinnatus also noticed a man whom he used to meet every morning on the way to the kindergarten, but whose name he did not know. Beyond these first rows there followed other rows where eyes and mouths were not so clearly drawn; and beyond them, there were layers of very hazy, and, in their haziness, identical faces, and then—the furthest ones were really quite badly daubed on the backdrop. Another poplar fell.

Suddenly the band stopped—or rather, now that it stopped, one realized that it had been playing all this time. One of the musicians, plump and placid, taking apart his instrument, shook the saliva out of its shiny joints. Beyond the orchestra was a limp, green, allegorical prospect: a portico, cliffs, a soapy cascade.

Nimbly and energetically (so that Cincinnatus involuntarily recoiled) the deputy city director jumped up on the platform, and casually placing one high-raised foot on the block (he was a master of relaxed eloquence) proclaimed in a loud voice:

"Townspeople! One brief remark. Lately in our streets a tendency has been observed on the part of certain individuals of the younger generation to walk so fast that we oldsters must move aside and step into puddles. I would also like to say that after tomorrow a furniture exhibit will open at the corner of First Boulevard and Brigadier Street and I sincerely hope to see all of you there. I also remind you that tonight, there will be given with sensational success the new comic opera *Socrates Must Decrease*. I have also been asked to tell you that the Kifer Distributing Center has received a large selection of ladies' belts, and the offer may not be repeated. Now I make way for other performers and hope, townspeople, that you are all in good health and lack nothing."

Sliding with the same nimbleness between the crosspieces of the railing, he jumped down from the platform to the accompaniment of an approbatory murmur. M'sieur Pierre, who had already put on a white apron (from under which his jack boot showed) was carefully wiping his hands on a towel, and calmly, benevolently looking around. As soon as the deputy director had finished, he tossed the towel to his assistants and stepped over to Cincinnatus.

(The square black snouts of the photographers swayed and froze still.)

"No excitement, no fuss, please," said M'sieur Pierre. "We shall first of all remove our little shirt."

"By myself," said Cincinnatus.

"That's the boy. Take the little shirt away, men. Now I shall show you how to lie down."

M'sieur Pierre dropped onto the block. The audience buzzed.

"Is this clear?" asked M'sieur Pierre, springing up and straightening his apron (it had come apart at the back, Rodrig helped tie it). "Good. Let's begin. The light is a bit harsh . . . Perhaps you could . . . There, that's fine. Thank you. Perhaps just a wee bit more . . . Excellent! Now I shall ask you to lie down."

"By myself, by myself," said Cincinnatus and lay face down as he had been shown, but at once he covered the back of his neck with his hands.

"What a silly boy," said M'sieur Pierre from above. "If you do that how can I . . . (yes, give it here; then, immediately after, the bucket). And anyway why all this contraction of muscles? There must be no tension at all. Perfectly at ease. Remove your hands, please . . . (give it to me now). Be quite at ease and count aloud."

"To ten," said Cincinnatus.

"What was that, my friend?" said M'sieur Pierre as if asking him to repeat, and softly added, already beginning to heave, "Step back a little, gentlemen."

"To ten," repeated Cincinnatus, spreading out his arms.

"I am not doing anything yet," said M'sieur Pierre with an extraneous note of gasping effort, and the shadow of his swing was already running along the boards, when Cincinnatus began counting loudly and firmly: one Cincinnatus was counting, but the other Cincinnatus had already stopped heeding the sound of the unnecessary count which was fading away in the distance; and, with a clarity he had never experienced before—at first almost painful, so suddenly did it come, but then suffusing him with joy, he reflected: why am I here? Why am I lying like this? And, having asked himself these simple questions, he answered them by getting up and looking around.

All around there was a strange confusion. Through the headsman's still swinging hips the railing showed. On the steps the pale librarian sat doubled up, vomiting. The spectators were quite transparent, and quite useless, and they all kept surging and moving away—only the back rows, being painted rows, remained in place. Cincinnatus slowly descended from the platform and walked off through the shifting debris. He was overtaken by Roman, who was now many times smaller and who was at the same time Rodrig: "What are you doing!" he croaked, jumping up and down. "You can't, you can't! It's dishonest toward him, toward everybody ... Come back, lie down—after all, you were lying down, everything was ready, everything was finished!" Cincinnatus brushed him aside and, he, with a bleak cry, ran off, already thinking only of his own safety.

Little was left of the square. The platform had long since collapsed in a cloud of reddish dust. The last to rush past was a woman in a black shawl, carrying the tiny executioner like a larva in her arms. The fallen trees lay flat and reliefless, while those that were still standing, also two-dimensional, with a lateral shading of the trunk to suggest roundness, barely held on with their branches to the ripping mesh of the sky. Everything was coming apart. Everything was falling. A spinning wind was picking up and whirling: dust, rags, chips of painted wood, bits of gilded plaster, pasteboard bricks, posters; an arid gloom fleeted; and amidst the dust, and the falling things, and the flapping scenery, Cincinnatus made his way in that direction where, to judge by the voices, stood beings akin to him.

ABOUT THE AUTHOR

Vladimir Nabokov was born in St. Petersburg on April 23, 1899. His family fled to Germany in 1919, during the Bolshevik Revolution. Nabokov studied French and Russian literature at Trinity College, Cambridge, from 1919 to 1923, then lived in Berlin (1923–1937) and Paris (1937–1940), where he began writing, mainly in Russian, under the pseudonym Sirin. In 1940 he moved to the United States, where he pursued a brilliant literary career (as a poet, novelist, critic, and translator) while teaching literature at Wellesley College, Stanford, Cornell, and Harvard. The monumental success of his novel *Lolita* (1955) enabled him to give up teaching and devote himself fully to his writing. In 1961 he moved to Montreux, Switzerland, where he died in 1977. Recognized as one of this century's master prose stylists in both Russian and English, he translated a number of his original English works—including *Lolita*—into Russian, and collaborated on English translations of his original Russian works.

VINTAGE INTERNATIONAL is a bold new line of trade paperback books
devoted to publishing the best writing of the twentieth century
from the world over. Offering both classic and contemporary
fiction and literary nonfiction, in stylishly elegant editions,
VINTAGE INTERNATIONAL aims to introduce to a new generation
of readers world-class writing that has stood the test of time
and essential works by the preeminent
international authors of today.